STORIES FROM THE MUSES

BECOME A BETTER WRITER

MARIA ILIFFE-WOOD

JB HOLLOWS

Introduction by
JULES SWALES

IW
Press

LIST OF AUTHORS

JULES SWALES

MARIA ILIFFE-WOOD

JB HOLLOWS

DEL ADEY-JONES

SAMANTHA HERMAN

JENNIE LINTHORST

AL MILLEDGE

MER MONSON

VÀNESSA POSTER

LINDA PRITCHER

LINDA SANDEL PETTIT

ANNA SCOTT

LN SHEFFIELD

SHARON STRIMLING

N. VYAS

First Published in Great Britain by IW Press Ltd 2022

ISBN-13: 978-1-8383330-3-4 (Paperback)

ISBN-13: 978-1-8383330-4-1 (e-book)

IW Press Ltd, 62-64 Market Street, Ashby de la Zouch, LE65 1AN

www.iliffe-wood.co.uk

For anyone who would like to be a better writer.

PRAISE FOR STORIES FROM THE MUSES

These writings came out of the quiet depths of the writers and communicated directly to me through feeling/energy. They stirred and awakened a recognition that only the heart and soul can make. We fall in love with reading stories so we may feel the movement of these inner energies. Laughter, surprise, love, fear, and tears all begin to dance within, as I read these enchanting stories. I delighted in coming under the wondrous spell of these muses. Read these stories with your whole being and be prepared to be stirred!

- Dicken Bettinger, Ed.D., psychological/spiritual educator, retired psychologist, Three Principles practitioner and trainer, co-author of *Coming Home: Uncovering the Foundations of Psychological Well-Being*

As I read this wonderful book, *Stories from the Muses*, it was like jumping off a cliff without a net. It is a ride that is exciting and, in a way, terrifying yet left me ravenous for more. I was tantalized with the perception of free falling into each Muses' story, and the rush of not knowing what my landing would be. It takes true courage to write with such transparency, depth, and openness. I was lured in as the story tellers opened themselves up and allowed me to peer deep inside. Such shared intimacy. Where they took me with their words was a visceral look into who they are. It was profound. I highly recommend this book and its approach for anyone who is wanting to explore them-selves through writing and in doing so become a better writer.

- Michael Monks, Actor, Director, Acting Teacher

Stories from the Muses is a collective work of true art. I imagine the excavation took extraordinary commitment, courage, and persistence. And then, to give voice to that energy, unseen and unspoken, is a triumphant gift to the writer and the reader. The quality of the writing is extraordinary, as each piece draws me into the raw experience of each Muse's truth. I'm blown away that this collection was written by students! The level of writing is accomplished and evolved. I appreciate the diversity of the voices, as in their co-existence and aggregation, they reflect humanity in its raw and purest form. Upon reading this, I find myself drawn to exploring my own muses. To know more of ourselves is to liberate ourselves. How brilliant to achieve this through writing. Bravo on creating this inspirational treasure!

- Lori Lenox, Executive Coach and Leadership Consultant at The Lennox Group and Corporate Edge. Bestselling author of *Ignite Your Life For Conscious Leaders*

Each piece in *Stories from the Muses* is a helix, a spiral that angles out to the reader from the core of its author. The challenge of writing requires each writer to delve into the DNA of their emotions and their life experiences, but then to process this personal knowledge through the energetic DNA of the archetypes the Muses represent. That is the beauty and strength of this collection of poetry and prose. It deepens the reader's experience of what was just read by revealing subtextual information about the process the writers went through to create these provocative pieces, pieces that intertwine writer and reader around what we have in common. Disquieting Muses, indeed! Bring them on! This is a marvelous book.

- Lisa Segal, award-winning poet; author of *Kicking Towards the Deep End and Jack Grapes' Method Writing: The Brush-Up Book*; teacher of Jack Grapes' Method Writing

Powerful. Thought provoking. Important. Every line is a winner. I've never heard of a book like this, and the whole concept is so interesting! I loved every word!

- Nancy Aronie - NPR commentator, author, columnist

Stories from the Muses stirs something deep within with every turn of the page. The intro tempted me with the mystery of what might come, and teased me to get more intimate with the muse energies that hide in the nooks and crannies of my being. As a reader the pieces were intriguing, but as a writer each chapter asks much more and reveals how confining the plane I've shared from has been. This book is something to taste and sit with, and then be in wonder of what my muses are dying to share.

- Kristy Halvorsen, World traveller and transformative coach

As a writer, and teacher of writing, I'm always searching for creative ways to access and to help students access the abundant energy of creation within them. *Stories from the Muses* is an incredible book, both a tool and a new way to explore. I certainly will apply these disquieting muses to my own work as a writer and a teacher.

- Justen Ahren, Author of *A Machine for Remember*, and Founder of Devotion to Writing.

Stories from the Muses passes the most important test of good writing: it captures the attention and engages the reader. Its intimacy, its raw truth, its purity of story in prose and poem invokes a deep connection with the individual authors. I've set aside beautifully written books because they failed to engage my caring. The opposite can be said for *Stories from the Muses.*

- Ted Box, Writer, President emeritus, Nathan Mayhew Seminars

In a time when free speech is stifled and we are fearful to voice our true feelings, *Stories from the Muses* is touchingly brave, flawed and reassuringly human. A book to cherish."

- Maggie Norris, Artistic Director & CEO The Big House

This volume brims with honesty. Selfish internal honesty offered without apology or fear. Distilled poetically at times, as fiercely as the prose, these are very short stories of inner life mirroring the archetypical energies that push and pull us all. The various muses have a chapter, and each of the writers expresses the impact of that role in their lives. Out comes the good and bad and the exultant or dismayed essential moments of truth for each. It is a powerful, emotional reading experience. If each writer's seven muse/archetype contributions were read as one, the book could be seen as a compendium of shimmering internal portraits.

- Richard C. Skidmore, Writer, Filmmaker

My personal favorites are "Messy" by JB Hollows' a beautiful evocation of childhood mess and sweets and "Unsung" by Al Milledge, a heartfelt reflection on the denial of fatherhood for a gay man. Relax, read, absorb - go with the flow.

- Declan Cooke, Actor and Elementary School Teacher in a US school in Tangier.

The energetic and intimate voices in *Stories from the Muses* captivate and inspire."

- Chanel Brenner, award-winning poet, and author of *Smile, or Else*

Stories from the Muses is a collection of raw, honest, and vulnerable writing exercises that inspire, provoke, enlighten, and entertain. There's something for everyone here. Each piece portrays an image, a moment, an event, or a story capable of changing lives. You may find yourself musing over your own muses, and thanks to the creative genius that is Jack Grapes—writing teacher to the writing teachers—new generations of writers (of all ages) get to bask in and grow from this deep, heartfelt work.

- Bella Mahaya Carter, Author, Writing Teacher & Coach

Stories from the Muses takes you deep into the human experience - this wonderful collection of writing exercises captures a moment in time - those seemingly ordinary moments when something or someone ends up being a defining moment in our lives. This collection of authors has written beautiful accounts from different perspectives of times in their lives. They take us into the minutia - the gritty and beautiful minutia of what it means to be human.

- Linda Ford, Master coach & Author

Stories from the Muses is an esoteric and artful collection of prose and poetry by a group of talented authors, who through answering the call of seven Muses, make personal confessions, declarations, and tributes. This journey of discovery wills each author to scrape off a protective patina. Either indulge in the journey of all the authors for one particular Muse, or perhaps follow the revelations of one particular author through his or her entire journey. Either way, their journey may become one of self-discovery for the reader as well.

- RJ Stastny, Author of *Falling Forward* and
The Guestbook at Asilomar.

Stories from the Muses is a book for everyone, and so it should be, but carrying a warning message about rollercoaster rides of emotion. A storyline of a child dancing carefree lulls me into safety until I'm shaken awake by the unmet sexual desires of a maiden virgin whose language is raw and honest. The journey through the Muses from different authors keeps the rollercoaster on its tracks and the reader unaware when the next drop or bend is going to hit. And that's what makes this read so addictive.

- Gary Jacobs, CEO and founder of FKC, a London advertising agency.

Stories from the Muses is a wonderful insight into how to work in harmony with Muses within your own body. This is a highly charged read with raw energy dancing off every page. The poetry and stories explore pain, joy, sorrow, love and all the other emotions in between. After reading this thought-provoking book, I was inspired to find the Muses within my own body and release their energies on to the page – the result astounded me.

- Anne Tattersall, Co-author of *The Book of Hope*

Stories from the Muses is an unexpected and insightful journey through the creative minds of writers exploring the seven disquieting Muses. In identifying and channelling the energy of these Muses, the writers bring to life the disparate parts of us that come together as a whole. Each Muse evokes such different stories and experiences from each writer and keeps us guessing as to which of these energies is activated within ourselves by their words. Reading these pages offers us the gift of inquiry and examination into our own Muses, showing us the scope and breath of the energies within and around us.

- R.P., Producer

This read is very deep, powerful and moving. I could feel the energy jumping off the page as each author completely opened up. After reading these stories I feel inspired to search for my own dormant muses and hopefully I can express and integrate them into my artwork.

- Dan Clorley, Pilot and Artist

I was deeply moved by this book. Each story struck me not so much in my mind as in my body. I felt transported to another's reality, yet reminded of the depth of my own. I can't recommend this book enough. To read it is to explore the depths of human experience.

- KC Hildreth, Executive Coach

Energy is central to the experience of reading *Stories from the Muses*. The writers clearly spent hours in emotional exploration to determine what each muse meant to them and conveyed that via the written word. Their greatest success is in conveying that energy to the reader. Rarely do you encounter a writing collection where the words simply reach off the page with a rich imagery and power that lingers. Each essay deserves time and reflection as they collectively challenge the reader's own conception and experience of muses, creativity and energy. Readers will leave this collection energized and with deeper insight into their emotional lives while the aspiring writer will find deep inspiration within these pages.

- Kirstin Hellwig, Sailor, Vagabond, Retired Consultant

Reading *Stories from the Muses* was a ride on an emotional rollercoaster that unapologetically exposed the rawness of the human experience. Gut-punching, heart-wrenching, satiating, and intoxicating, I found myself anticipating the next muse, craving to know more about each author's lived experience through their writings. I found the Muses a wonderful container for unveiling universal and personal narratives that brought me right into an author's intimate experience of love, loss, pain, triumph, and hope. I highly recommend this book!

- Regina Klenjoski- Choreographer, Artistic Director, Founder, Regina Klenjoski Dance Company

CONTENTS

PART VI
MUSE SIX

PART VII
MUSE SEVEN

FOREWORD

Stories from the Muses is another anthology of personal essays written by me and thirteen other students who studied Jack Grapes' Method Writing with Jules Swales. The Disquieting Muses is Level Four. If you read A Different Story, the first book in this series, you will know that we had to sit and write with nothing on our mind. Write like you talk, and the other tonal dynamics we learned at Level one were the foundation of every piece. This time, we had to find various muse energies within our own body and let the muse do the talking.

It was a surprise to me how precise that location turned out to be. My Huntress was in my throat. The Crone energy between my ribs and my heart and my Child danced all over my body. She was not to be pinned down! I've never given birth, so I wasn't sure I even had a Mother Muse in me. This was also true for several of the students, yet there she was, an inch behind my solar plexus. Once we'd found the location, then we were to write from that energy.

It was not as easy as it sounds. Very few of the Muses were how I imagined them to be. You will see what I mean when you read these stories. You will find there are almost as many different Muse energies as there are authors.

This class operates in a different way to most of the other levels, in that the exercise is not prescriptive. After we've written our pieces for each Muse, and read them out in class, only then will Jules talk about the various Muses and their energies.

The book is structured to emulate the classroom experience. It's split into seven parts, one for each Muse, but we won't tell you which Muse it is at the outset. Instead, each section contains an 'epilogue' where Jules will talk about the Disquieting Muse that you have just experienced and the exercise.

My recommendation is that you read the stories in each part and see if you can feel the energy of the Muse and where it might be located in your body. Before you read the epilogue, see if you can guess which Muse you've just experienced. Each part only contains one Muse - no matter how it might seem!

I am delighted that Jacqueline (JB) Hollows, has joined me again in this endeavour. We are joined by twelve other authors, some of whom are already published, others are first-time authors. The quality of writing is so high, you will not be able to distinguish between the first-time authors and the 'pros'. They hail from both the United States of America and the United Kingdom, so you will find a mix of American and English in this book.

Once you've read the book, perhaps you will give it a go. Decide on a Muse, locate his/her energy in your body, then write from that energy and see what happens on the page. You might be surprised by what shows up. I know I was.

Maria Iliffe-Wood

INTRODUCTION TO THE DISQUIETING MUSES

BY JULES SWALES

A big thank you to those who have contributed their work to this project and a huge brava/bravo to all those who have taken Level Four of my Method Writing program.

Method Writing Level Four—Disquieting Muses

So, what are the Muses? They are the seven expressions of feminine or masculine energy. On the feminine side, they are Child, Virgin/Maiden, Mother, Siren/Seductress/Whore, Huntress, Crone/Hag/Witch, and Medusa. On the masculine side, they are Child, Virgin/Youth, Father, Siren/Seducer/Whore, Hunter, Wizard/Sage, and Medusa. Each week of Level Four, the writer picks one of the seven Muses and writes from the energy of that Muse.

Oh, cool, I get it, you might say, but for anyone who has traversed through Level Four, there is not an ounce of: *cool, I get it* during the seven weeks. This level is full of surprises, stumbling blocks, frustrations, tears, and revelations. It is often quite grueling for the writer, but in the most magnificent of ways. One could say the eight weeks of the Muse Level serves as another chapter in the writer's Hero's Journey.

One of the challenges for the writer doing Muses is being too literal. We think about muses and archetypes and often believe they are the same thing.

> Archetype: The original pattern or model of which all things of
> the same type are representations or copies.
>   Websters Dictionary.

This definition says that an archetype is the original thing, and everything after that is a copy. In the Muse exercises, we look behind the archetype of Hunter **to the individual energy of the Hunter Muse for each writer.** Every student, every writer, every person has their own unique Muse energy. Finding and exploring these often-disinherited parts of ourselves is what can be so exciting about this level.

For those who think: *Ah, yes, Gestalt.* No, this is not that. Gestalt is about finding the voice in the body and letting it talk. Muses are all about **energy**. Sometimes, when told: *Write from the Medusa Muse,* the student will go straight to his or her head / intellect. They will recall all they know about Medusa. How she was one of Phorcys and Ceto's daughters, and how Perseus severed her head, and how drops of her blood turned into snakes (to this day it is believed this is why there are so many serpents in Libya) and how Perseus used the anger of her gaze to turn armies to stone. Anyway, the student will think: *I'm going to conjure all my anger and fury onto the page.* This could be a fun adventure for the writer but will render the writing limited and overt. There is no surprise in writing that is overt by its very nature and in its content.

I have heard more than once a student's surprise when they located their Medusa Muse energy only to find she/he has no fire or fury but is tired and weary. That is the journey of Level Four - Disquieting Muses - to disquiet and explore these dormant energies inside.

One of the beauties of this exercise is that there is *no getting it right* because energy states, Muse or otherwise, are subjective. The invitation of this level is for each writer to find his or her personal *Muse* energy for each of the seven Muses and to bring the energy of her or her personal Muse to the page. The student is not writing about the archetype, and not writing as the archetype, they are looking behind the idea of archetype to the energy of Muses.

As the energy is located and unearthed, it will alter basic sentence structure as it effects, distorts, heightens, and changes the writer's voice, both in tone and diction. This takes patience and perseverance as in each of us are dormant and sometimes lifetimes' old energies waiting for their day on the page.

> *Archetypes/Muses are part of the universal language of storytelling and command of their ENERGY is as essential to the writer as breathing.*
> Christopher Vogler - The Writer's Journey

Sometimes students will say: *I haven't had a child so how can I do the Mother Muse, or I'm young so how can I do the Crone Muse, or Goodness no, I've never been a seducer type of person.* My reply is always a version of: Don't be literal, locate the energy in your body, and let it write you onto the page.

Some of you may be wondering: *How does this help with writing?* Great question. I'll let Christopher Vogler answer that.

> *The archetypes/muses can also be regarded as personified symbols of various human qualities. Like the major arcane cards of the Tarot, they stand for the aspects of a complete human personality. Every good story reflects the total human story, the universal human condition of being born into the world, growing, learning, struggling to become individual, and dying. Stories can be read as metaphors for the general human situation with characters who embody universal, archetypal qualities, comprehensible to the group as well as the individual.*
> Christopher Vogler - The Writer's Journey

Each of the pieces in this book is a result of the writer/student exploring themselves in a new way. Some of their Muse energies have been easy to access, while others have taken more perseverance, more writing, more tears and more calls with me. The students have shown great tenacity and a profound willingness to be open to their individual creative journey and individual relationship with Creative Genius.

PART I

MUSE ONE

1

THE SQUIRREL KING

BY LINDA PRITCHER

I'm a pretender. I've always been one. I've wondered the difference between one thing and an-other, between one reality and another, between childhood and adulthood with its loss of mystery and magic, between my world and yours.

"Yo ho, you jackdaws and adventurers!" I shouted into the deep blue wildness that stretched in every direction. I'd dropped the rope from the highest branch of the tallest tree. It was as high as I'd ever climbed. Here, the Land of the Carrion Crows had given way to the Seven Crowns of Heaven.

Climbing had taken all day, but there I was beneath the stars. Now, I was queen of my realm, pretending into being, all that is. And tonight I would be the seven-crowned soul mate in an ancient legend, looking out with my kaleidoscopic spyglass on eternity.

The rope had come to rest at the feet of my Squirrel King. The ermine collar of his fitted woolen cloak, the color and scent of wet earth, was fluffed to reach his hollowed cheeks. Those cheeks were now devoid of blue birds and night sky, but his eyes still warmed like ancient forest amber. The Persian carpet beneath his feet, tapestried his future, woven from his past. He stood priest-like and serene.

The jackdaws had settled in neat rows along the lower branches, heads tucked within their ashen grey wings. A tiny citron colored glass had nestled in the crook of a gleaming bent bone that lay moonlit beside the looped rope coil, quiet as a snake at dawn before stirring.

We'd been days in our journey. Our meeting had been in haste. The map agreed to, the vows exchanged, the path secured by the twined tendrils of solitude we had shared.

The earthen hatch door obscured by fallen leaves had been left open, unattended and waiting. The portal called.

"To adventure!" I said into the night, into the land of pretend where I am queen, into my destiny. As I slipped by the stars and plummeted earthward along the rope's length, the pale shadow of Jupiter's rising moons extinguished the lights of the Milky Way.

The sweet kiss of the Squirrel King would be mine.

2

MESSY

BY JB HOLLOWS

I'm messy. And chaotic. It's what the world needs. I bring movement, where there is order. I bring simplicity, where there is complexity. I bring honesty, where there is deceit. The room electrifies when I'm in it. I open eyes. I bend ears. I tug at hearts.

Wind circles storm up a mood as I walk. Dust, dirt, debris fill the air with smoke screens. Blinds the sense out of the norm. Disrupts the usual. Messes up the standard.

I gobble up each mouthful of life's gifts. I stuff my mouth with fistfuls of chocolate cake days, and jelly tot moments. I lap up buttercup milk and glug down dawn lemonade. I take what I need and play with the rest.

I'm satiated, then I'm not. I'm delirious, then I'm not. I'm exhausted, then I'm not. Shame does not touch me. I'm born into the world's sin, but I'm not of it. Chipped red nail polish doesn't brand me a whore. Broken promises don't condemn me a flake. Changed moods don't label me a diagnosis.

Fairy tales and rainbows rule my days.

Unicorns with glittered horns feed from my pudgy, open hands.

Sunlight and sandcastles colour my hair.

Fear hides in unexpected places: dark corners, spiders' webs, the bathtub in the moonlight glow. My warm blanket disappears the angst, comforts me against a reality I'm not yet ready to face. Morning light brings a fresh start. Night terrors shrink back into their dirty cloaks.

The call of music dances my feet. Spontaneous regardless of venue. I twirl and twist to an inner tune. My toes wriggle free from socks. My arms stretch to catch the wind. My body sways with supple limbs.

I play with grown-up masks, taken from the wooden crate at the foot of the bed. The one that's painted blue with green sea horses and pink shells.

I place them over my sweet, plump face.

I act the part while interest holds.

First a donkey, now a prince. Then a Jester, now an angel. Then a long whiskered cat, now a green-eyed monster.

Expectations don't stick to me. I'm too fresh for that. Still shiny from mother nature's womb. Untainted by the stench of disappointment.

3

SPACE OF LOVE

BY LINDA SANDEL PETTIT

"Happy Birthday, dear Luke," I said. Luke's Mama had dimmed the lights of the circular chandelier in the modern dining room. A bundt cake, sprinkled with powdered sugar, stood on a pastry pedestal. The flames of four candles, twists of green, yellow, red, and blue, flickered in Luke's wide eyes, the shade of ferns. A portrait of awe. His cherub face was framed by a fresh brush-cut, Papa's handiwork.

Birthday presents in colorful wrap were stacked behind him. A paper plate, cobalt blue, embossed with 'Happy Birthday' in red and white calligraphy, waited for his cake and vanilla ice cream. A giraffe binkie, a pacifier, rested sucker side up on the table next to his two-year-old brother, Alex. A painting of a lone bison on the plains was visible over his head. "Happy Birthday to you," I said and finished the song.

Luke unwrapped his presents—a projector to turn ceilings into space observatories, and a three-foot-tall wooden rocket ship. Luke was enthralled that the rocket ship had an elevator. His Mama plugged in the projector. The darkened great room glowed with the majesty of the Milky Way.

"Blast the rocket ship to Jupiter, Grammy," Luke said. His voice was urgent. He strained on tiptoes. Head in the stars, his thin arms were raised to the ceiling. His bright eyes were fixed on Jupiter, his favorite planet.

"Let's imagine a blast-off," I said and stood in my flower-sprigged black dress, to join his dream. "No Grammy." Luke said in protest. "Not imagine, make it real." He started to cry. I was flustered. I would do anything for that child, that small boy, that love, but I felt my grave. My shoulders squawked, yet I bent down, hauled up the three-foot rocket ship, and aimed it toward the planet next to the smoke detector on the moon.

"Count down with me, Luke, honey," I said. My arms trembled with the weight of the ship. Our eyes plastered on Jupiter, we chanted; "10... 9... 8... 7... 6... 5... 4... 3... 2... 1... blast off!"

"Houston, we have lift-off," I said and hollowed my voice to make it sound official. "Grammy! We're headed toward the future!" Luke said. His little arm slipped around my leg as he leaned his head on my thigh. I ruffled his hair. On an orbit to a distant star, we slipped the love of space into the space of love.

4

UNSLUNG

BY AL MILLEDGE

A generation has passed; I didn't recognise the painful loss of my own 'never were' kids. Retrospect is the only lens. I didn't want to be the dad in the Larkin poem. Ready to fuck up a life or two, with my victim forever present. I didn't have the tools, no one has.

I couldn't have kids by accident. There was too much time to consider the logistics, the process, the outcome. I'd be the unwelcome gay dad, at the school gate in Thatcher's Britain. I could see myself give credence to the looks and the tittle-tattle; my kids being folded into my battle with the world. I wanted them because I wanted them, not for show or political clout. I wasn't ready to be a test case.

The space my nephews and nieces took up, in a heart meant for my own, was a pump of blood to a sallow place. I roughed them up on our Saturdays together. I rattled my box to find my own kid to share, in the game, in the dust, down on the floor. I brought to those days all I'd needed someone to be for me. I didn't know how to Dad, but I was one of sorts. It's factored in, programmed, on call waiting. I'd just overridden the ease of it. We've learned together, they are parents now. I'm still left to wonder why I don't have my own.

5

APPOINTMENT IN SAMARRA

BY VANESSA POSTER

My dad will live six more years to be one hundred, or he will not. Morgan always said, *worrying is like praying for something bad to happen.* I pray for bad news every day, when I look for trip hazards, evidence of cognitive decline, low oxygen levels. If I plan every moment, weave the yarn of every possibility, I know I can outwit the angel of death.

Every day he navigates dangers of standing up from a chair, walking to the bathroom, beating his heart. When I wake up at night, I check the camera I have set on my dad. I look for movement. When I see breathing, I can fall back to sleep. He's alive.

Henry, the pig down the street, snaps at beet greens I hold out to him. The sign taped to the fence says that Henry is leaving today to go live with his brother, Tamale, at a farm a few towns over. He's too big for this small enclosure in a front yard in Redondo Beach.

His curly tail wags like a dog's as he grabs for greens. He eats them all. I wonder if the whole Tamale story is fake, like telling a child that the dead dog was sent to a farm to chase the ducks. I want it to be true that Henry will stretch his stubby legs in farm-yard sun and cuddle up next to Tamale at night, to share the scratchy warmth of his brother's hide. I want Henry to live.

I am weak and buffeted by my dad's moods, my moods, and X-rays that show he has two more broken ribs from a fall in the middle of the night. A fall I did not hear. A fall he hid from me, lying to me when I came down to say good morning.

Henry snorts and sighs, lies back down in the shade, oblivious to his fate. He will either be on a paradise farm with Tamale or in someone's tamale. His fate, my father's fate, are out of my control. I will try to cultivate radical acceptance, or not. Maybe I'll just go eat a tamale.

6

I AM THE DANCE

BY MARIA ILIFFE-WOOD

"Stop dancing!" My mum said.

I was seven years old and stood on a wooden chair, high above her crouched head, as she tried to pin the hem of my dress. My new dress. Pink gingham with sleeves that came to my elbow and big pockets for all my things. The sun came through the window beside me and swathed me in a ball of sunshine. This dress was all mine. Not a hand-me-down from the family that lived two doors away. I could see the top of her auburn hair with a white crown in the middle and imagined the pins in a tight grip in her mouth. "Stand still." She said.

How could I? I could see the world from this mountain crest. I could see the top of the morning with my whole life ahead of me. I could see my first day at school, how the other girls would swoon and coo and admire me in my lovely new dress, like they never had before. My heart beat in joy and wonder like it never had before. My feet jiggled like they never had before.

"No." I said. "I am the dancer and the dance and the music and the rhythm of life. I am freedom." My mum laughed like she never had before.

She didn't do that.

That was my imagination, my wish, my prayer. She never did

laugh. The light in her eyes and the joy in her heart had been clouded by the harshness of the material world. The reality floods back, but the dream remains, the new dress remained, the ability to imagine a happy world remained, the vision to see what had never been seen before remained, to see beyond, to see the good, and to see the joy in my heart. That all remained.

And the dance remained.

There is no way to stop the dance.

The dance remains forever.

7

I AM THE TIGRESS

BY N.VYAS

I play drums in my mind
twirl to make-believe music
the tango I dance and salsa too
I love my body
how it moves
all on its own
to think I spin the world
on its axis would be silly
it happens all on its own
like these words
flood out of my head
like the ocean's roar
the shooting star's wonder
the rainbow's pot of gold
I am the tigress
I own the jungle where I roam
my heart rumbles
the earth quakes
sunshine sparkles
moonlight glows
clouds float away

off I fly on sunset's tide
my magic carpet ride
above the pyramids
golden tops open
I drop into the center
of my inner sanctum
filled with honey
ensconced in emerald beauty
I am
where violet hums
and melodies are made
mine is made of preciousness
threads of gold and silver weave
into a blessing
mine to receive
with dandelions tied in my hair
timelessness born around my wrists
the milky way wrapped about my waist
I step back into the fold
and wonder
what's next

8

WHY I STARE AT THE CEILING

BY JENNIE LINTHORST

I woke in the night again with dread – an existential mix of *have I done something wrong* and *does anything matter*? Did I forget an imagined medication my son should have been taking for months now? Stress dreams visit me often—I can't find a classroom for math that I know is in my schedule; and from my years in a modern dance company, I can't pull my hair back into the bun that is required. My costume isn't in place, and the music is about to start. I remember waiting, under our glass paned kitchen door, for the sound of my mother's antique Mercedes convertible to chug into our driveway, bringing her home with a stack of books from law school. Miss Lattimore, our house-keeper, sat at the kitchen table, chain-smoking to *The Price is Right* on TV, grumbling under her breath about our mess. I was always waiting, waiting for someone to come home, waiting for someone to pick me up. Nervous, I was unprepared for the next thing. I was parented mostly by babysitters. Beth, who left before I could remember, then Jeanne, who left to become a flight attendant. I remember sobbing. My pigtails mashed into her waist. Angela drove me for a time to all my required activities, then left to become a UPS driver. Then there was Caroline who moved in with us, those final years of my mother's illness. She lived in the twin bedroom just off the kitchen. I watched her fall in love and leave to marry a pilot in the air force. She packed into her suit-case secret moments, only she saw in my mother's final days. Memories of our mother disappeared like the scent of her perfume. It was small moments I needed most—someone to help me put hairpins into my bun, someone to shop with me for my first training bra and help me through my first menstrual cycle. I have spent my life preparing for the next thing, never quite sure I can handle it, relieved when it is over. In my dreams, I walk empty hallways, breathless that the world has moved on without me. I have lost the red sash of my costume, the stage is lit, the music is playing, and it's time, it's always time.

9

WAKE UP CREATIVE GENIUS - IT'S SUNDAY!
BY LN SHEFFIELD

I wriggle myself under the covers. A desperate attempt to stay in that sleep state. Sleepy and dopey. Soft sounds whisper, sips of early morning strong tea. I'm comfy and cosy, warm and sweet. I love the morning snuggle. Mmmmm. A soft murmur leaves my dry lips. The deep orange glow of sunshine creeps under the curtain edges, teasing me to wake. I resist. I want to keep this feeling forever.

Yet it's time to rise and shine, explore the day. I'm curious as to what it will bring. A delight of colours to play with on my palette. Laid out like a buffet of treats. My eyes twinkle at the very excitement of the feast before me. My fingers tingle with a sense of urgency. Ready to pounce. Ready to create. Ready to get playful. Ready to allow the flow of curiosity.

A deep itch, a need to scratch.

My belly rumbles with an instant need to be filled, as my pen comes to a halt. What if creativity dries up? What if I have nothing left? What if creative genius sleeps all day on a Sunday?

The thought fills me with dread. Tears well up and overspill, dampening my cheeks, pausing in the creases of my dimples. One moment joyful and fun. One moment, tears and heartbreak.

One moment, wide awake. One moment, overcome with exhaustion.

A myriad of moments. A wave of emotions. A rollercoaster of life crashing through me. Pulling and dragging in one direction. Tugging and tossing in the other. Throwing and shoving all over the place. The test of time. Can I stand tall? Can I sway in the breeze? Can I bounce from one thing to the next without a care in the world?

Ping-pong, ping-pong, ping-pong. Rinse and repeat.

Bouncy like a tiger with all the joys of spring. Creativity and rest. All in one day. One hour. One moment. Letting it all bubble up. Letting it all out. Letting the world see.

Free. Vulnerable. Soft. Hard. Tucked up. Wide open. Giggles. Tears. Pain. Sweet, sweet joy.

All in a day's work.

I want to shout from the rooftops - I trust. I'm wide open. Take me. Wake up creative genius - It's Sunday!

10

WAITING FOR YOUR LOVE

BY DEL ADEY-JONES

I'm tired of living in a future that never arrives. Waiting for you to end my pain and make the longing go away.

The ache is unbearable. A yearning that can't be filled. An insatiable hunger gnaws away at my insides. I'm a mistake. I should never have been born. My very existence hurts people. People hurt me. I don't know where to go. I can't run away. I'm not brave. I pee my pants if you just look at me.

No love, no comfort, no sweetness, no joy.

Pennies in my pocket. That's all I need. Sweeties become my source of love. Fragrant sticky toffee. Sustenance for the soul. I stuff my mouth with the sugary confection. One more and the emptiness will be gone. But the end never comes. The bottomless pit of need cannot be filled. Shame is all I feel. Unending pockets of shame. Malignant, inoperable shame.

Fear is my companion. Fear of the distorted and contorted faces. Fear of the unknown. Fear of the known. Fear of the screams that pierce the silence. Fear of the deranged, lascivious eyes that follow my every move.

Yet I love you. A deep, unfathomable love. A love that ties your heart to mine. A love that threatens to kill me if you cease to exist. My nightgown clad body lays trembling against the cold slate floor. I wait for morning to come. I wait for the clink of keys turning in the lock. I wait for your love.

11

SELENE'S CHILD

BY SHARON STRIMLING

I howl at the moon, and the moon flares back.
In her light, I run.

I chase owls, dodge fireflies, thrash my toes
on brambles and stones.
I scream my laughter, mud
my thighs, and wail my misery - or joy.

Branches quiver, tease me from on high.
I look up, feel small,
and weep
on the moss at their roots.

I race wildcats in my dreams,
wake to a spider's tickle, catch my breath
at the spring pop
of a crocus.

I twist grasses into giraffes and hippos into stars.

I came to this world over the moon.
Excited for birth, excited for death, excited
for life. Excited for touch, excited for sight,
excited to be kissed,
and played with and taught.
I came tasting and testing
and spitting and loving.

I came to this world soft, and shell-less
and unconcerned.

I came to this world to take it all in,
the wild that begged me here,
the existence that held me,
that shielded my skin,
guarded my heart.

I came to this world to take it all in.

And I did. I took it all in
the moments of hunger,
the breast and the heat,
the soft of pure cotton, the light
in my eyes. I took it all in
the bars on the crib, the walls smooth
and white, the distance from me to
another. I took it all in
the storms that came, the windows
that shook. How we stayed dry
when the squirrels didn't, the earthworms
didn't, the mitten I dropped
in the yard
didn't.

I took it all in
as little stranges,
little by little,
turned to little normals.
But I knew.

I knew the stranges, as I knew my toes,
as I knew the earth
beneath them, as I knew the wind on my skin.
And I turned on the stranges
as I slept
on moss
as I raced the moon
as I bled on rocks.

I howl at the moon
and the moon flares back.

I wear fur on my arms, and taunt snakes with
my hips. I race owls
and language and rules.

I twist grasses into wolves,
then wrap them to my feet
and run.

EPILOGUE - CHILD

Webster's definition: a young person, especially between infancy and puberty.

We would imagine that when the writer picks "Child" for their week of "muse" writings, they might lean into memories of childhood. For most of us, there is a plethora of material lingering in the folds of our past from which to draw. But that would be too literal an exploration for the writer and might limit their writing.

Method Writing exercises are not subject-centered. We are not interested in starting to write with a story/idea. We let the exercise direct the content of what we write. This is particularly evident with "Muses."

Curriculum directive: *Each week you're going to pick one of the seven muses and write from its energy. There is no order, but don't do the same muse twice. Note the title of Level 4 is "Disquieting Muses." You will give each muse energy state inside you his/her voice.*

There are no examples in the Method Writing book as to what a muse might sound like. This is because one person's "Child" energy might be quite different from another's. The wonderful surprise for many writers is in discovering what the energy state of their muse conjures up on the page.

You will see a bit of a thread through some of these writings. This occurs more often with the Child and Mother/Father muse than with some of the others, but still there is a stark contrast between them. How in pieces like Lucy's and N. Vyas' there is no thread of sameness, or how Del's "Muse" energy is written from struggle and fear, and others from wonderment and exploration.

I can assure you that all the "Child" muse energies and hence pieces were not floating on the surface of the writer's awareness. They had to get quiet, dig a bit, explore, look away from the obvious. The key is not to write from the first place you arrive at when you think of the "Child" muse.

I wonder what your "child" energy would say if you were to meet her/him on the page.

Curriculum directive: *One of the mistakes people make is finding the energy and then writing what they think about the energy. No. Don't do that. Find the muse energy and then let the energy itself inform the writing.*

Be curious, look deeply, and ponder questions like: *What is behind the words of where you first arrive? Where in your body does your "child" energy live?* And again, don't jump at the first answers. The whole point of this level is to invite the writer to discover themselves in a new way, and to commit that newfound entity to the page.

Jules Swales

PART II

MUSE TWO

12

BROWN PAPER

BY SAMANTHA HERMAN

It was obvious to anyone looking on that the two girls hunkering down in break time were up to serious business. She, the friend, had been given the book to make sure she knew the value of her gift. I, on the other hand, thought the gift an annoying impediment.

Girlhood confused me. How that thing could be seen as a prize, a commodity. I used to sit in my right on sisterhood circles, discussing how we would overcome the patriarchy, one home-made reusable tampon at a time. No conglomerate was finding its way into our pussies.

There was political power, but what the hell did that mean. It, the big IT, was a socio-political hindrance. I had read that in Spare Rib. Huh, well, I thought it a practical one too. I sat in the same weed strewn playground, where the must be a lesbian netball teacher had yelled at me, poring over the brown paper-covered book, amazed that my friend valued the IT and would never ever countenance giving her IT to Simon Fleury, even if he was the prettiest boy in the lower sixth.

Truth was, I was painfully shy, like blushing from nose to toe deepest beetroot, anytime I had to speak to a group of more than two. Make that one, if a boy was involved. I had practiced snogging my pillow, but really, what was the point? I wanted a different persona, a way to overcome the beetroot and to feel like I was in charge buster. And I had a bargaining chip... or so I thought.

Hence the brown paper-covered book, devoted to the best way, and the whole experience, of ridding oneself of IT. Strange suggestions, such as having some pre-prepared snacks, selecting favorite musical tracks, guidance on depilatory products. Oh, come on, I wanted the nitty gritty.

This was not some romantic sunset, never come up for air kiss... I wanted to liberate myself and finally feel in charge of my destiny. Nobody was taking anything. I was divesting myself and hoping to transform in the process. I had already offered IT to the aforementioned Simon Fleury and rudimentary plans had been hatched to bunk off school and meet five minutes from his house.

The chosen day happened to be a bit sludgy with rain, and as I waited by the iron railings, my hair began to frizz. I waited and I waited, and then I went home. The next day I heard Simon boasting in the halls about the date he had yesterday with LuLu, a soon to be top model, hanging out by the canals in Camden Town. Yesterday's frizzy hair framed my beetroot pancakes, as I rushed to the girl's loo for a conciliatory morale boost from my friend.

She hadn't taken the book from her bag yet. It had a chapter on dealing with disappointments. I felt most womanly, as I shared at least that one ubiquitous experience.

13

BUT NOT HIM

BY LINDA PRITCHER

In the semi-darkness, the bottle spun. It glinted in the sharp crease of light that pressed through the slivered edge of a closed basement window. Beneath me linoleum tiles, smooth black and emerald-green squares, covered the floor.

It was the tail end of summer, hot and humid. We'd been restless with discovery, raiding the neighborhood of its fun, and our well had run dry. So there we were, crouched in the semi-darkness, the bottle spinning. The linoleum, cool against my skinned knees, was a hard contrast to the hot lava swell inside. A fan whirred in the background, letting loose a swirl-wind of emotion, then relief, as the bottle mouth spun by me again and again.

Too afraid to look up, my eyes had been following a tiny ball of lint skittering across the floor, pushed one direction by the fan, another by the force of the spinning bottle, this way and that. I was too afraid the bottle would point to me and not him, this way and not that, to someone else, not him.

Not the him I wanted to be my first kiss. The him I'd wanted since fourth grade, when kisses were from parents, aunts, uncles, and grandparents, always on the forehead, always on the cheeks, never on the lips. In the movies they were on the lips, red or deep pink ones, sometimes violet ones. They were sweet and gentle or full and passionate.

The bottle spun and spun, and spun again.

"Not him." I murmured into the hot summer sun. I opened my eyes to the heat on my face, to the scarlet rose bushes, to the dry prickly grass, to the summer almost gone, to the left-over churn and burn of the hot lava in the cool of that basement. But not to him.

The washcloth-wrapped ice cubes on my forehead had melted to a dribble across my chest and sleeveless eyelet blouse, leaving dark soaking spots of coolness. I felt the lounge chair's plastic lattice strips pressed into the backs of my thighs. But not him.

My empty glass lay on its side. Lemonade stains stroked the pages of my opened book. But not him.

I felt Ginny's tiny doll-hard body tucked alongside me on the lounge chair. The hot breeze caught the soft edges of her skirt and ruffled her bright blond hair, this way and that. But not him.

14

HUNGER BEFORE THE FEAST
BY JENNIE LINTHORST

I hurt in my yearning; a kind of suffering that calcifies into layers of age, tucked away in drawers, rarely opened. The daily barrage of duties flattens me, sucks oxygen from my fire. But the yearning, the yearning still waits, yearning pounds a subtle drumbeat underneath. How do I not hear it for so long? It's an old melody deep in my hips that surrenders to wonder, to electrical senses, a tingle that follows pelvis to breastbone. I have forgotten how my husband and I used to slow down, get away for a night. There were rituals of slipping into white silk, the feel of my skin in his muscular hands as we swayed to music, his beard on my neck. *I need more of this*. I told him last night. More of this — slow touch of his fingers, my nails whispering on his back. More of this escape where yearning builds. This is the space that heals me, the space that strips away time, the space that cradles my vows, forces us to look eye to eye at twenty-four years of time. This is the space where I can soften jagged edges of this past year, know that I am still his girl. Space I can receive his safety, before I open and give, and give, and give, and give. I know now this is sustenance in these stale walls of a pandemic — gentle caresses, skin on skin, hunger before a feast. Thank God, yearning is still there.

I can taste its fruit. I can daydream about another night ahead, closing our bedroom door, Dave Mathews and The Rolling Stones. I will tell him to linger at the sweet in between. Here, in the slow sway of our dance. Here, where I am most alive.

15

THE HYMEN'S TALE
BY LINDA SANDEL PETTIT

As a maiden, I checked my wild nature and sexuality to preserve my cherry. Later, I discovered that the hymen was but a crescent flap of embryonic tissue; a remnant that male-dominated religions imbued with moral meaning.

I had two nicknames in high school: 'Miss Advent' and 'Sassy'. Translation: irreverent and rebellious.

Miss Advent stuck, after I perched an Advent wreathe on my head during a study hall. A school photographer snapped an iconic photo. It freeze-framed a teenager, her hourglass body costumed in an asexual Catholic school uniform, her waist length red hair crowned by a Christian symbol of expectant waiting.

"Sassy" was the gift of the journalism teacher, a nun, who first noticed my writing. I called her Mom. A nuclear power plant of a woman, she luxuriated in adolescent female rebellion.

Mom was maternal pan del cielo, my bread of heaven, sky bread, holy bread. After I left for college, to major in journalism. Mom was assigned to a different high school. I missed her like the night yearns for the moon.

During my first Christmas break, I drove to her new home. A

drafty echo chamber of a convent, in an old Polish neighborhood, near downtown Detroit.

The convent smelled of oiled floors, aged wood and old women. I sat across from her on a faded floral sofa that sagged under the ghosts of countless guests.

Breathless, I filled her in on my collegiate classes, accomplishments, and jobs.

She interrupted and said, "I want to hear, Sassy, about your dates, your pleasures, and your fun." I stared at her kind, rounded face, framed in the dim light by a white wimple and black veil.

"Tell me how you opened your senses to the poetry of your soul." She said. The cuckoo hid in the clock on the wall. "There's nothing to tell." I said. Her crone hand cupped my wrist. I squirmed under her gaze and enigmatic smile.

I kept every letter Mom wrote me. One is penned on a piece of stationery that quoted George Eliot: *'Tis what I love determines how I love.*

George was a woman, Mary Ann Evans. Known for her realism and psychological insight, she shrouded her Victorian era writing under a male pseudonym. To avoid waves. To breathe. To publish.

Intuitive. Creative. Sensual. Fierce. I secured my wild poet in plain brown wrapper. I cloistered my erotic heart. I barricaded sensuality, sexuality and passionate creativity behind the façade of a pleaser.

My life. My life as a young woman was the tale of a cherry preserved in a sweet syrup of constricted beliefs and false values. My life as an old woman will be no hymen's tale.

16

EASY PREY

BY DEL ADEY-JONES

I remember the night I died. Diane and Richard had taken me to the pub. We'd found a table in the corner, away from the crowd. The hushed whispers and furtive glances told me I'd been noticed. I was out of my depth. A shy, self-conscious teenager. A thin layer of puppy fat, my only defense.

His eyes bore into me. His prolonged stare let me know he had noticed me. Like a hunter stalking its prey. Biding his time. I kept my head down. Afraid to look up for fear my eyes would betray me. My neediness and emptiness on full display. The heart on my sleeve beckoned the advances of those seeking easy prey.

He made his way across the bar. Handsome. Black-haired and blue eyed. The father figure I yearned for. "Do you still live up at the Hall?" He said to my sister, as my eyes met his. His piercing gaze left me in a state of awe and confusion. "Yes." She said.

Lying in bed, I heard tires move slow through heavy gravel. An engine purred to a stop. A car door closed with a quiet thud. Footsteps approached my bedroom window. I drew back the curtain and his face emerged out of the darkness.

"How old are you?" He was sitting at the edge of my bed.

His back towards me. A lit cigarette hung from his right hand. The smoke curled up towards the ceiling. The room was dark, but for the dim light cast by the bedside lamp. A spent bullet lay next to the alarm clock. The stench of his alcohol breath hung heavy in the air. Rumpled sheets lay in damp disarray. I lay there lifeless, discarded, deceased. My suicide note, signed with a drop of blood. "Fifteen." I said.

I'd like to blame him for my death, but deep within, I know I was complicit. That my naivety and neediness made him do it. He was right. It was my fault. I shouldn't have met his gaze. I shouldn't have led him on. I shouldn't have let him in.

17

THE MAN IN MY KITCHEN
BY SHARON STRIMLING

I dreamed of him from the empty space,
the space of gentle nothing,
where it was good, and I was good,
and anything could come.

A space that knew itself before itself,
that knew perfection, knew peace.
Empty space that started out soft,
budding, honest,

that embraced skin as it embraced sky.
That drove life to meet life
in mind, then heart, then body,
through honor, matriarchy, tribe.

I read about a society, long ago,
with shamans who guided their young
in sacred circles—out of the sacred empty,
and into their sacred form.

Within my cringe was envy.
For I grew up in the suburbs,
where norms sat cross-legged
on silent mystery. And still.

I knew the fertile empty.
I knew the gentle nothing.
I knew the blessed union,
and dreamed.

I dreamed of him, from the space of
gentle nothing, where it was good,
and I was good,
and anything could come.

18

ALL AND SUNDRY

BY AL MILLEDGE

I'm tipped to the top with the vibration of man. No one else, except me, cares what I need and I'm glad of it. It's packed in like sardines. I'll parade it around until someone with an appetite realises it's their lucky old day. Come at me, I've got enough to go around, enough to jump about, enough for one and all and all the sundries. It's prime, and it's free baby. It's my Yang, but it's yours for as long as our knees hold out. Tremblers, nuzzlers, pity all the puzzlers, come rummage in my dungarees, I'll be busy with the panderers and I'll even take the philanderers.

My Yin, if you're bothered, went South on Monday last. I'm certain never to see the arse end of it again. It wasn't any use to me, anyway. Kept on trying to take over the show. I'd wobble, a little worry wobble, that I was going to fuck something up, and before I knew it, Yin would win out again and shut me down, with the speed of a tranquiliser dart.

Well, now it's gone, binned, left with its stubby little tail between its legs, tunnelled its way out and left a big pile of sand at the entrance, slid under the fence while the dogs ate their dinner, tipped over, cast asunder, locked out, never to darken my door again.

I'll roll in the hay on my own if I have to until someone sniffs me out. I'm-a ready. I can feel sherbet in my toes, in my fingers, through my whole body in waves. My tank is brimmed. I'll explode onto the circuit like a gated stallion. Let me at 'em. You won't need to bring your enthusiasm, just come as you are. Veracity, audacity, and elasticity are my university. Pile 'em high, I'll make 'em cheap.

I'm the seed of a rambling rosebud, the same seed as the petulant old grump, so come and catch a load of it before it goes off, shows off, cracks off, peels off, buggers off.

19

THY WILL BE DONE

BY MER MONSON

These ancient breathing women wake and stretch beneath my skin. They take me by the shoulders, as I look each of them full in the face. I get to be as I am now, untethered. I've come out from behind my own skirt. There is no going back. I am ready to let these goddesses of every feminine face have their way with me. I open my mouth.

Ha! It's never been about a man, has it? It's been you, all of you, the whole time, my true loves all in a row. It's your daggers and nipples and lullabies and bones pushing up through the dirt of my world. It's you strumming my vocal cords and growing my babies. It's you leading me on the dance floor, heating me up and swirling me into adventure.

Run your river through me, beloveds. I will not stand in your way. Sway my hips, spread my wings, and loosen my tongue. Wrap my arms around the thundering trees. Fill up my veins with oceans of honey. Plant a vision in my womb and grow it to glory. Crack me open and storm the floodgates in the center of my chest. Place a jewelled dagger in my grip and beat my hammering fists. Throw six-inch heels and lipstick on me, for God's sake, if you must.

And at the end of the day, come dance with me in the firelight, as we move our feet to the rhythm of the fireflies and the drumbeat of the apes. Melt the earth's madness with your feast of all-consuming grace. Milk me for all the love I'm worth, until the fire dies, and you lay me to rest in a field of lilies.

I am back at the door of beginnings, suspended and swimming in the alchemy. There is nothing left to smother or shame. I am terrified, awake and shining. I step off into thin air.

20

SEX IS ALIVE IN ME
BY LN SHEFFIELD

I feel horny. I don't want to write that. I don't want to feel that. I don't know what to do with the feeling. It's been hidden away for so long. No needs, no desires, no longing to be touched. No wanting to be loved. Brushed under the carpet. Swept away. Yet it over spills like a river bursting its banks, after a heavy rain pour. Gushing, over-powering. Running wild from the inside out.

I'm scared. I'm too honest. I'm too open. I feel it all. I wish I didn't. My heart thuds loud in my chest. It pounds like the thudding of an elephant through an empty jungle.

I want to kiss every inch of her body. Want to touch and caress her. Want to please her. Tickle her and take in her scent. I want to feel her naked skin against mine, hot and sticky as we lay together. I want to twiddle my fingers through her hair. I want to talk all night long. I want to stare at the stars with her. I want to nestle into her as she wraps her soft arms around me. I want to be so naked with her, that I discover mysteries of my own imperfect body.

I want to cook with her. I want to fuck with her. I want to scream out loud as we orgasm together. I want to be inside her. I want to know how she feels. I want to know how she tastes. I want to know how she smells. I want her so fucking bad. My body tingles with a long forgotten ache. I can't contain myself.

Her fingers tease me, caress me, rub me. Butterflies that flutter so hard against my tummy, it's painful. An excitement, a nervousness, an anxious feeling trapped inside. My desire throbs hard in my clit. Hard & fast. A need so deep my body writhes and buckles beneath me. And I haven't even met her yet.

It isn't me. It's alien. I can't be loved. I spread my toast with only the tiniest amount of butter.

I'm unloveable. I'm unfuckable. I'm untouchable. I'm not good enough. I'm too afraid. I'm too honest. I'm too open. I can't let anyone in. Yet it's written now. Set in stone. Known through the ages. A sex that is alive in me.

21

ALL OF THIS

BY ANNA SCOTT

The vast star-filled skies above me are pale in comparison to the space within me. This space expands and contracts on its own, for what is needed. One moment it holds the birth of a baby, the next, the grief of the loss of that same child.

The pink of me is as pure as that of the first rose blooming on its brown stem. Don't let the thorns fool you or worry you. They are part of my perfection.

The purple bearded iris journeys its contorted bulb through the earth and emerges in its own time to have us gasp at its beauty. I have to be present to see it, for its show is only brief - like life.

Who gets to decide on the length of life?

Who is the time manager who begins and ends life?

Who is orchestrating all of it?

I would like to meet this person.

The sweetness of me is like honey dripping and sticking to the shelf and jar. Golden bees work their antennas and create this sticky wonder.

Depth. I am a free diver, holding my breath for three minutes, as I plunge to the bottom of the lake, understanding what it is to fill myself up and be able to hold the beauty of life.

I am magic. I am made like an oak tree. Growing from this brown round thing with a funny looking little cap.

Music dances from my voice, touching and uniting all around. For a moment, allowing us to forget our sorrow and pain, and just be.

Unity. I am the air. The space between notes. I am the empty space in the photograph. The white canvas whispering, inviting the paintbrush. I am the pen waiting for your hand to pick me up, to form lines that become vowels, consonants, words, and finally, a masterpiece.

I am hot sticky sex. Sex that has you feel electricity run through your body and light up a city. Sex so wonderful you cry for God, grateful to be in your body.

I am the tongue that licks the melted ice cream off the hot brownie. Teeth that bite into the juicy strawberry. Fingers that get to wipe the plate clean and not miss one bite of that orgasmic food.

I am blessed I get to be this simple human.

EPILOGUE - VIRGIN/MAIDEN/YOUTH

Webster's definitions:
Virgin: a person who has not had sexual intercourse, a person inexperienced in a specified activity.
Maiden: an unmarried girl or woman.
Youth: a young person, especially a young male.

A young person who hasn't had intercourse and/or is inexperienced in something. If we think about maiden/youth, we imagine an adolescent who is beginning to explore the space between child and adult. There is a wonderful yet often naïve vigor when a human already feels they know so much, yet they have so much still to know.

The first time I did the Maiden Muse exercise, I felt I knew, without doubt, the energy and life of my maiden. Her energy was going to be dark, and I was so ready to meet her on the page. I made a person of her in my mind, black nail polish and eyeshadow, multiple ear piercings, and a general disdain and sense of hopelessness. I thought I could feel her energy. But it was the energy of my intellect, and this can often derail the Muse exercise.

When I sat down to write, like all purist method trained writers, I cleared my ideas. I wrote the first sentence with nothing on my mind. To this day, I remember the shock as I felt the energy of the Maiden Muse inside. She was as light and hopeful as a feather. I felt the flutter of her tickle in my stomach. If I had a picture of her, she would be dragonfly-like. Shimmering blue and green wings and I kid you not, a smile as wide as Texas. She had more hope than my brain knew what to do with.

That is the invitation of a) Method Writing and b) the Muse exercise. To find ourselves on the page in new ways. Writing, if we let it, can be the panacea to all that ails us, and the Method Writing way is the best I've found to date.

Curriculum Directive: *The Muse exercise is not about creating a character on the page. If you write a character, you are not digging deep enough. It might take a bit of time to locate the individual Muse energies, so give yourself more time each week to write. And remember, if you think you know the muse energy - it's not that. This is about locating what you don't know.*

When you read Mer's "Thy Will Be Done" you will be taken on such a ride, you might wonder how on earth could the writing arrive where it did? It was because the writer was doing the exercise. Those last lines: *I am terrified, awake, and shining. I step off into thin air.* The thrill and fear of Maiden are palpable in those words. As with Linda Pritcher's "But Not Him," the spinning bottle, the first kiss wanting, the little doll tucked alongside the narrator's body.

All the writers in this book know how to look to the unknown when they write. They leave inspiration to amateurs and they trust imagination or Creative Genius to help them deliver on the page.

Jules Swales

PART III

MUSE THREE

22

I WANTED TO GIVE WHAT I HAD NOT GOTTEN

BY JENNIE LINTHORST

Our neighbor's Peruvian Pepper Tree drapes her ribbons behind my bedroom window. I like to pretend that it's a Weeping Willow of my Tennessee roots, remembering how they called to me in my youth, planted next to ponds, riverbanks, and lush green grass. Those sweeping leaves dripped like tears during a rainfall. Somehow, nature understood the depth of our human condition, created a majestic crown to pause and see the rise and fall of our days. I knew at a young age that I had an old soul. After the slow death of my mother, I honed a keen sense, a light behind my eyes that could peer into darkness. I was not afraid to hold a hand of the dying, to ask more questions of love abandoned, to pick up my friend at the end of her driveway while her alcoholic father lay passed out on the floor. I wanted to give what I had not gotten — the gentle hand stroking my back, stroking my hair at the end of a long day, stroking the embers of good enough and it will be okay. That's all we really want — a kind place to heal. Nothing felt better to me than filling that void for my friends. I learned to listen for the hollow places that needed sustenance. I learned to cook their favorite meals, build a house to invite them in with warm colors, warm beds, warm fireplaces to sit out their tempests. I learned how to read them the right poem, how to play the perfect song, how to pause their pain for hours with a pallet of paint, an empty canvas, and play. When I was pregnant with my son, I rested a hand under the curve of my belly, ready to hold him, ready to lift the weight of him, ready to understand the voyage of this bloodline. I can see glimpses of my eyes in his grown face. As he moves into manhood, I need someone to sit with me under the Weeping Willow, someone to witness the tears of this passage, someone to tell me I have done enough, and that he will be okay.

23

CHILD, YOU KNOW (THE HAWK'S SONG)

BY SHARON STRIMLING

Tear skies with your screams.
Bind grasses with your confusion.
Throw your questions to the river,
and your dreams to the lake.

Break things,
then watch them re-grow.
Plant things,
then let them surprise.

Lie down.
Close your eyes.
Take care with your questions.
See what comes.

Ask only the questions the rivers haven't answered,
the grasses haven't answered, the skies haven't answered,
and the ones you're sure,
you're sure, your heart doesn't know.

Then come. Come sing your answers
to my heart. If they're funny,
I'll laugh with you.
If they hurt, I'm your lap.

Come. Place your hair
in my fingers
and your body in my care.
Come. Lay under my eyes,

where I can see you,
and the hawk above your head,
the coyote to your right,
the rapids to your left.

I'm your hawk, but bigger.
I'm your hunter, but everywhere.
I'm your tree over the river, fallen just right,
with footholds the size of your being.

Come. Lay under my eyes
until you find your answers
in the river,
your dreams in the lake,

until you know the hawk's song,
the coyote's tracks,
the quiet curl of the rapids.
Then go.

24

THE ANCIENT ONE

BY LINDA SANDEL PETTIT

In the modern doctor's office, the seats were COVID-19 spaced and pandemic scarce. A twenty-something maiden, her expression sculpted in kindness, jumped to her feet as I entered the door. She offered me her seat, a long grey bench.

"Thank you," I said. "But I'm all right." I wondered: who did she see?

I thought I would be at home in my end-game skin at age 67. I thought I would sun myself, in gardens of succulents, and slither on heat-bleached trails. I thought I would bob in a river and wait for a waterfall to spray me free, against the boulder of death. My dumb luck—I could feel it coming on; another skin was about to be shed.

The memory from long ago flashed behind my tired eyes. Rustic and wild, the dwelling had been unoccupied for months. With the metallic screech of a rusty oil derrick, the door swung open to my push.

I saw the snakeskin straight away. Draped between a heating duct and a mahogany railing, on the second-story balcony. The skin was gossamer, a mother-of-pearl filament, at least six feet long. It shivered in a draft. Dead. Left behind. An echo.

I marvelled at the sheer will it had taken, for a snake that size, to wiggle out of a too-tight skin. I wondered how vulnerable she had been, as she had crawled away on virgin scales, not yet toughened to splintered wood and to the scratch of dirt.

"That's a powerful omen." I said to my companions as I pointed to the skin. "Snake medicine. The energy of transformation."

It was not on my bucket list to shed another skin as an older woman. Yet, here I am, in labor. I kneel in an ache on all fours, head bowed to my breasts and exert a guttural push to midwife a new voice, a poet's voice, the voice of real. It's a bloody thing. I have dangerous questions. Will my wordsmith daughter inhale wind into her lungs? Will the bluish girl cry fire into my body? Will she bleat into the air of a polluted world? Will the antique fibers of my golden vocal cords revive into their destiny?

It doesn't matter if the child survives. At my age, it's a safe bet we will die sooner rather than later. Our acapella voice will reverberate over the galaxy and join the chant of infinity.

I'll die, though, to raise her until I go. I know she'll bring joy to my left-over days. Maybe we'll feed a hungry mouth or two, or three, or more.

Little did the maiden in the doctor's office know. She offered her seat to the Old One, an ancient mother-in-waiting.

25

MIDDLE

BY SAMANTHA HERMAN

I am missing a middle.

Hollow, empty, nada, nothing to look at friend, travel on. The middle was once there. It had a brief dance in the sea spray, sun glistening on its perfect navel. Now it is a dug out burrow and holds courgettes and potatoes in rich deep earth.

It is a mass of never-ending root tendrils, which bed in with veins and cells and ligaments.

I am a tree.

My limbs are splayed out like a climbing frame for everyone's exploration, feet in face, nails in groin. I am hollow, so it doesn't count. My womb is lined with forest fur. I grow there. I grow in my third eye. I envision from my crown. I extend tendrils of love - flow from my heart through my fingertips, to the page, to the sunset, to the warm ocean waves.

I create.

Rest in my armpits. You will find sagacity and safety.

Rest on my legs. You will find strength and purpose.

I open the orbit. Fly through dusk colours eating the soil.

Rest on my wings, you will feast on the multi-facet dream.

Bite too hard and coldness so swift will chill your bones to crumbs.

Disrespect and feel the scorn of shame.

This is a necessary rupture, the clumsy move of a fawn.

Deep buried seeds of fossilized potential await the perfect fit at the perfect time. Experience will shape and reveal the soul.

I am the compass.

The middle, the end, the portal for all affection, the balm for all suffering. Unconditional love is in my gift and to have that I offer my middle. Whilst you are in my domain, I will shape, hone, and squeeze the essence. A remembrance will reside in my hollow after fledging, an imprint of lifeblood to be cherished and valued when you have finished your time with me. I have no need of ownership. I have given my middle. You will love as best you can. It is of no consequence; I follow my own bidding, the bidding of the missing middle.

26

A TRICKLE OF JUICE
BY AL MILLEDGE

Can't tell a crocus not to grow in the dirt.
They pop out wherever there is a shaft of sunlight.
Dilapidated and deprived, the road grimy.
Houses with saggy roofs
for folk with saggy humanity
in a world with a saggy middle

Few brothers get out.
Garbage hung about until it rotted through the floor.
I slid out on a trickle of bin juice.

Tagged trucks with shot out windows
jumped over fences to dodge drive-bys.
A sandwich on the fly with the flies.
Art. Workout. Dinner.

Low riders, down siders, cart pullers, vat stirrers.
The dead ones were slow or forgot,
or rode the system past the last stop.

We didn't try to work out how to get away
'cos we didn't know it'd be different nowhere else.
The music we were fed was polished shit,
even if we did all spit along
and believe for a moment.

Too busy in survival
away from our locked-up mothers,
forged a crew of our own.
Created some rep along the way

Then you don't have to fight for every inch,
every score, every breath,
every break, every time.

A pin burst my bubble; I can't go back.
Hardest and easiest decision I ever made,
to live life.

27

THE SACRIFICE

BY ANNA SCOTT

I feel the whip hit the horse.

I have a parched mouth and a dusty face. My clothes are soiled and torn from inside out. My underwear elastic no longer works, so a safety pin holds the threadbare fabric together. The dirt in my belly button has accumulated so much, I can feel it stick out when I rub my belly.

My thigh muscles are like solid rocks. My feet are calloused, so I wear a protective shield for the miles I march. My boots are worn and fitted to my feet, like there is no separation between the two.

My silver scope is in the right pocket of my heavy leather jacket. It was handed down to my grandmother. She gave it to me when I was chosen for this role.

My bow is on my back, with a tan quiver of well-used arrows. When I finished my training, I was given this case with my initials branded into the leather. As well as the name of the woman I serve.

I hate to lose an arrow. I used to gag when I'd pull one out of a bison, or a man. I would often be grabbed by the wrist and end up being wrestled to the ground.

I got good at being aware of the last breath.

Twisting the arrow out is an art form. I lost so many because of my impatience. I wouldn't feel the tip under the rib. I would yank too fast and it would break off. Now, if I am patient and feel for it, I can slip the tip under and away from the rib. My awareness of the arrow and flesh has deepened.

I love the rush of energy in the chase. I love the fear. I love the moment when it is over. Eyes change from bulging out, to a dropping back in the skull. It is like they give themselves to me as a gift. It is a sacred moment.

I bow my head in reverence to the sacrifice. I think I am the winner, but sometimes I wonder if it is the other who has really won.

28

DEAD PEOPLE'S WORDS

BY VANESSA POSTER

"I can't throw this journal away." John says.

We are sorting through his dead wife's things. We have been married six months. To combine our households, we must read the notes, diaries, college papers of our dead spouses and decide.

We honor our dead in loving each other. It is a pilot light of honor. Burning, not consuming.

I dreamt last night I was wearing my dead husband's shirt. The maroon long sleeve I wear when it's chilly. Morgan holds me. I cry, wanting to love him just one more day. In the dream, I take off the shirt and embrace it, naked bosomed. Holding empty cooling cloth with no living heart.

I don't cry awake anymore.

A parent can love two children. I love two men.

With Morgan, it was a word dance, a balance of understanding. Together we taught classes for women, on how to find love, living the example of it. He spoke his advice, his truth, in the lower register of a man, talking from testosterone awareness, translating into female vocabulary.

With John, I silence his word flow with a kiss. A lawyer: practical, solid, fierce, devoted. When I walk into a room, I warn him that I am sparkling, so he can continue to breathe when he turns around.

It is a practice, like writing, or yoga, to learn how to feel this happiness. I watch fire from the edge, darkness behind me, sparks in front of me. I don't want to drop the shirt into flame. I keep shelves and shelves of Morgan's journals, his agency of living, meaningful only to me.

John and I sort through boxes and files and photos: trash, recycling, waste. It should all be burned. Then we see a spark of a human we each once loved, had dinner with, sat with in an emergency room. A handwritten word in someone's shape of letters, uniquely theirs, holding a piece of them.

"Let me put that here." I say and place her journal in a plastic, weather-safe box.

29

IT NEVER STOPS, THIS JOB CALLED LIFE

BY JB HOLLOWS

It never stops, this job called life.
Every waking moment is dedicated to the cause:
Sing, eat, sing, fly, sing, rest, sing, mate, sing.

Day in, day out, I die.
I find ways to worry, to serve, to restore,
to listen, to teach, to fret,
to nurture, to try.

I fly to the moon, bone cold and naked,
to bring back the stars.
I scatter their cool light in your hair, on your breast, in
    your mouth.
So that you thrive.

I capture the sun, scorched skin and blisters,
to harvest her beams.
I trickle its goodness over your toes.
So that you shine.

I burrow the earth, deep, dark and sticky.
Fingernails black, red hair matted, choked on
the nutrients sucked into my lungs.
I bathe your skin in its healing power.
So that you are strong.

Your first joy is the essence I live on.
I carry you with tender ferocity.
My heart beats in time with your breath.
As time wears on my body crumbles, my will strengthens.

You stop seeing me. I never stop.
You take me for granted. I never stop.
You scar me. I never stop.
You lie to me. I never stop.
You laugh at me. I never stop.
You ignore me. I never stop.

You try to kill me in oh so many ways.
Every day in every action with every indifference,
your knife sinks deeper into my tender flesh.
I never stop.

A smile from you courses through my veins,
plumps out my skin,
beats a drum in my heart.
I never stop.

A token from you showers joy on my desert,
wakes the flower of my womb,
tingles my bud.
I never stop.

A moment from you,
acknowledges my existence,
refreshes my purpose,
I never stop.

The moon presses her face to my window.
Drenches me in her balm,
soothes me to sleep.
Another day is spent to protect you, my son.

It never stops, this job called life.

30

FIELD OF DREAMS

BY LN SHEFFIELD

I'm a worrier, through and through. If I don't have something on my mind, I feel vacant, empty, like my life has no purpose. Like my insides are being put through a shredder. My world seen through a mist; it blocks me from grabbing life with both hands. It's beyond my grasp. I can smell it, sweet like candy. I can see it, glistening like crystal rainbows. I can hear it, tinkling and shrilling, bursting my eardrums with pleasure.

I can't reach it.

A hammering soundtrack of drums beat loud in my chest, as the worry imposes deeper. I'm greedy for a snippet of life wrapped in sunbeams. I dream that I could live in a silky galaxy made of marble. It will never be. For I'm a worrier, through and through. It's in my blood, in my nature, in my genes. That once youthful face, with its cheeky smile, is hidden amongst those permanent worry lines and wrinkles. I'm forever fearful. A deep, dark knot of anxiety resides in my belly, like a ball of hot fire.

I wear worry like my favourite pair of ripped jeans, which I'm afraid to throw out. It's a chink in the armour of human emotion. I'm broken. Unfixable. I crack on, taking each day in my stride. Forcing down the despair. Squashing it like it means zilch.

When the worry takes a well-earned rest, guilt kicks in. I'm not good enough. I don't do enough. I don't care enough. I'm a wide cracked open woman who feels it all. A sensitive little flower who has no clue how to balance this harrowed life.

Pass me my shovel, so I can dig an early grave. I need rest. I'm like a lizard skitting about, trying to hide in the shadows.

I move fast through the ripe green field of doubt. My favourite dwelling. I crave the day my field of dreams comes into existence. The day I can have it all and then some. The day I'm no longer faulty at my core. I crave it all like a thirsty teenager, lapping up love for the first time.

I'm a worrier, through and through. I fear it all into existence, just to worry it away again. I am a master of my own destiny.

31

IF I WERE IN GOD'S SHOES

BY MARIA ILIFFE-WOOD

Life is a board game, played by a higher power that has the ability to create millions of universes and for whom an eternity of perfection would be the most intolerable tedium.

This almighty being sits in an ivory tower and, for entertainment, watches pawns like me scuttle around like ants as we try to cope with the blows that get rained down on us. I'd laugh all the way to the bank if I were in God's shoes.

And if I were in God's shoes, I'd make life a whole lot different, I tell you!

I'd make sure that people know it's a game, that they can choose to be happy or sad, positive or negative, up or down. That they can handle whatever life throws at them, no matter what.

I'd make sure they were equipped to deal with every trauma. I'd give them the ability to solve problems, no matter how huge. They'd be able to imagine anything, even things that don't exist yet, like world peace, and then bring it into existence.

I'd ensure that no matter what, they can always come back to a place of calm and stillness, a place they call home, a place where they 'know' without having to know anything. I'd make it so that people can be happy, no matter what their circumstance, and where every wrong could be made right. I'd ensure that love was everywhere, in the scent of a rose, in the eyes of a newborn baby, on the pages of a book, in the satisfaction of a job well done, in a quiet moment. I'd place it so that it can be found whenever it's looked for.

I'd make every single person a piece of creative perfection, each one unique and with a particular part to play in the world. I'd give them the capability to notice and value their differences, so they can see how the world adds up to a perfect whole. And I would give them the free will to be what they want to be, because who wants to live in a world where everything is pre-determined.

If I were in God's shoes, this is what I would do.

Oh yes! I see that's what she did. And she called it...

Humanity.

EPILOGUE - MOTHER/FATHER

Webster's definitions:
Mother, a female parent
Father, a man in relation to his child or children
(I find the subtle difference interesting.)

The definitions sound about right and what most of us would think when we hear the words "mother/father." But as with "child" it would be too on-the-nose for the writer to think about "mother/father" in the classic sense and write from there. However, even if the writer did do this, there would still be an interesting outcome on the page. This is because each writer would connect with their individual energetic space, and that affects the rhythm of the sentences, the beat of their writing.

> Curriculum Directive: *You do not have to be a parent to write a mother/father muse. If your intellect is mulling around with notions of parent, you are being too literal. Expand your idea of mother/father, use the energy of your body, follow it and write your first sentence. And remember, there is no right way to do this.*

In this chapter, Jennie touched on her mother's death, but she didn't get lost in the story. She stayed with the energy, and we were able to get a sense of the writer as a child, a mother, a soul. It's all there because she stayed focused and wrote from the energy, not the story.

Method Writing teaches you how to be a storyteller, not just tell a story.

The first line of Al's piece, *Can't tell a crocus not to grow in shit,* is a superb opening line and says so much. Ponder it and see if you can feel the energy behind the sentence. It might be a hot, intense energy, but it could also be an energy fueled with a deep poetic melancholy. Only the author knows what the energy is inside, and where it lives in their body. We don't discuss the nuance of the energy, although I might ask the student where the energy lives in their body.

> *Archetypes/Muses are part of the universal language of story-telling and command of their ENERGY is as essential to the writer as breathing.*
> Christopher Vogler ~ The Writer's Journey

The key to the muse exercise is to lessen your ideas and thinking about the muse and to focus on more of an inward experience. Not inward, as in therapeutic internal reflection. But a getting quiet and an acute listening to the framework of the body.

If you question whether you can feel energy in your body, do this: Lift up your arms, palms up, and hold them there. Close your eyes. Can you feel inside your hands? If not, then hold your arms up longer, you will feel something. That is energy, your energy, and it has a language.

Jules Swales

PART IV

MUSE FOUR

32

HELLO BEAUTIFUL

BY MER MONSON

I am afraid of my own parts and pieces, holding them at arm's length and under the covers. I do not see all the hands that keep me from making my own body's acquaintance. I bury myself from the waist down, a gritty mudslide of shame caked across my chest. I do not know my curves and crevices need to breathe. I cannot taste the deep down flavor of me, the flickers of God beneath.

Then I am touched by adoring faithful hands and I know. I know why they try to snuff it out and pray it into a corner. I know why they tell a thousand stories to dim the blaze. Silly people. Silly stories. Silly church. I wake, bright eyed and hungry for friendship with my own texture. Hello beautiful. Hello God container. Hello point and curve, soft and hard, fire and ice.

And now, I get to be naked, with or without my clothes. I get to feel air and silk and water on all my surfaces. I fall into the emptiness where life just gets to be as it is and full of breath. I move. I rest. Something is unleashed now the covers are gone— some out-breath, some mystery, some river of relief.

I feast on beds of mangos and artichokes and let all the tiny fish swim between my toes. I taste the coolness of celery juice, the knots in my man's biceps, the fresh rosemary and dill on my warm baby potatoes, and the dark wild blueberries filling up my cup's arms.

I love and make love with my golden speckles and spots, my crinkles and my missing parts. I wear them like jewels that shine out of my eyes. I fall, behind my back and on my back, into ever bluer skies of wonder, ever deeper oceans of satisfied want, and ever wilder meadows of power and grace. It is not too little too late. I have found the secret.

Nothing can unwoman me.

33

GRAVITY

BY SHARON STRIMLING

Bass rhythms pounded through the floor,
into my thighs, my hips, my heart.
My arms extended, spun force.

Eyes closed, head back, I raced
the rotating reds, blues, greens that swam
through the thin flesh of my shut lids.

My mild faded, and gravity was born.
Gravity spun out from heavenly bodies
unbounded, unrestrained.

I spun on hardwood floors,
sweat-soaked by music, by movement, by life.
I pulled the watching, pulled the wanting, pulled the
    intoxicated,

pulled the yes.

Pulled, captured, and held,
as moon to earth, wind spun life to center.
I spun beyond universes, union, and dissolution.

I pounded, thundered, crashed on shores.
I fell under, below, behind, and over,
ocean, wave, and undertow.

The rhythm slowed, and gravity dimmed.
Heaven fell back to quivering thighs,
thighs fell back to earth.

I touched my thighs, their wet, their worn,
the blisters of my toes, the tired of my years.
I touched the heavy of my sex, the ache of my soul.

I touched the gravity of my heart that couldn't pull it all;
that tried when I was twelve, then twenty,
then every day since.

Gravity that pulled the wanters,
the lovers, the loss.
I ran my fingers through my wet hair,

up the base of my neck, pressed my weight
to the slow spun lights above, then back to the floor.
I fell to earth's pull, palms down,

stretched the bend from my back,
and let my heavy go.
I saw a watcher through my open calves,

caught his glance, played toss with it, and smiled.
A never-gone spark breathed me out
as my hips rose to his gaze.

34

THE YES GIRL

BY JENNIE LINTHORST

I used to believe I would die young like my mother. There was a ticking clock counting to age 39 filling me with a fuck-it-all atti-tude–*cancer will get me anyways*. I was different from the usual college student wanting to break the rules. I wanted to consume life's terrain all at once, live it hard on a risky edge, taste the bitter and the sweet. I was the yes girl who would ditch classes in upstate New York, hop on a plane to New Orleans to catch last days of Mardi Gras with old high school friends. The one to order one more round of shots, one more deep talk about what it all means, one more kiss to keep it alive. I was the one who'd still be sitting on a Key West dock at sunrise, opening another pack of camel lights with a lukewarm beer. I lived like I was saying a slow goodbye, hoarding pieces of a life into my memory. Men were a playground of catch and release. I lured them into corners of parties, locked eyes, had soulful conversa-tions probing their character, their past, their cracks, then nurtured them with my southern drawl. It's kind of shocking to me now, as I sit here, a rule-following, white-knuckling mother and wife, stuck in suburbia remembering that freedom. I didn't die at 39. I've almost made it to 50. There is a sexy kind of freedom waiting for us in under two years when our only son leaves for college, crowded with visions of renting our house and living in Barcelona for six months. But will my fire still be lit for a bit of danger? *We'll figure it out,* my husband always says when my fears stomp on our dreams. He fell in love with the dreamer in me twenty-four years ago on a San Francisco rooftop, listened to my plans to save the world with the arts. I consumed him with that same fever. I need him to remind me of her, remind me that there's life beyond these safe, manicured streets, remind me that the clock is ticking, and it's okay. No, it's important to say, *Yes.*

35

LOVE'S ORIGINAL PROMISE

BY MARIA ILIFFE-WOOD

Part I

Touched by a sliver of God's light
darkness falls away.
Softens the bones
of my existence and
susurrates
love's sweet melody.
Emboldens my soul.

Joy
Expands,
encapsulates
all of what is.

Sweet
is the eye
that sees,
beyond
the constraints of virtue.

Nectar
is mine for the asking
imbibed
with grace and gratitude.

Nourished is my soul.

Ambrosia thaws
deliciousness
weaves
a silken heartbeat.

A trillion universes
swim
in my consciousness
I float
in a paradise
of love's original promise
fulfilled
in the bliss
of a tender moment.

Part II

I weep when my soul flounders
in the harpsong intensity
of emotion,
when I feel the shame
bequeathed
by the cretinous minds
of dogma and ritual.
Yet I rise
bidden
to my blessed wholeness.

36

WONDER WOMAN

BY SAMANTHA HERMAN

To begin with, it was a game, scoring the amount of attention we could get. Flexing inherent impulses, we wondered at this newfound power. We didn't know what was going on, just that our bodies were primed for action and demanded release. In this game, one needed chess-like strategy, subterfuge, and deception with a dash of roulette wheel recklessness.

A game predicated on one-upmanship, or should that be one-womanship? Those few moments when nothing mattered other than the power we held. When we pretended that butter wouldn't melt in our mouths, relishing the ability to give sweet satisfaction or punish with painful frustration.

As I explained, it was a head game, not a body game. The body was secondary, the net to the ball, a container not an actor. But I'm getting ahead here, just to be clear; it was always a contest between girls. Get it. Nothing to do with those boys and their ridiculous todgers. It was the score of who were counted to be beautiful, sexy, seductive that I was keeping, that we all kept truth be told. Who was going to be the champion at leading by the short and curlies. We revelled in the power to suck into our bodies, to absorb, even, we fancied, to transmute ecstasy into a power that marked our place in the world. A strategic game of body chess... sacrifice this part for that part. I was so busy perfecting my skill at beguiling, that I missed the lessons on the rest of womanhood. That I had a responsibility to my centre, my soul, the me of me.

Once the innocence all dried up, there was a different score being counted. Cognisance was slow to bud and the law of unintended consequences was always waiting for the right time to jump in. My recalcitrant nature would not be tamed, and little could I fathom that self-immolation was the price I would be called to pay.

Fleeting encounters maybe, but they left their mark, even when long forgotten, those mindless boys and their cocks had somehow deposited donations which waited like unexploded torpedoes, ready to wreak destruction in an overlooked moment. A loss of sensitivity so acute that I became barren to myself, a foreigner in my own body, a stranger to my sweetness, a refugee from my strength. A pariah to my wonder woman.

37

MANIFESTO

BY N. VYAS

I'm too much for most. So I've believed most of my life. Too much feeling. Too much intensity. Too much desire. Too much. But I love my *too much*. I mean, why not be *too much*?!

As for the fools who bought into this too much nonsense, well, their loss. I don't need 'em. I don't need anyone. I've got everything I need on this solo journey 'cause remember, I'm too much, all on my own.

There's glorious freedom on this path. Loneliness doesn't factor in. It ain't my thing. Besides, there are plenty of delicious dalliances to be had with no strings attached. I can do what I want when I want. I can play all day long. I can eat up the world and enjoy every flavor on offer.

Why bother with a conventional life full of pretense? Oh, no! It ain't my thing. I will not give up my liberty — not for love nor money, not for comfort nor security, not for naught. It's the silver linin' that floats my boat, all the way to heaven, with no anchor holdin' me back.

A glimpse into my world is all it would take to change everythin'. The endless possibility, the adventure — pure exhilaration.

I'm talkin' about alive, my people. Pure joy races through my body every freakin' day. That's my thing! I'm committed to one thing and one thing alone, my sovereignty. It's what I live by, thrive by, and will die by. I mean, without it, count me dead already.

38

ON THE SHIP

BY VANESSA POSTER

I hear noises, a voice,
music banging with rhythm and silk;
a pulling, dancing.

Sailors watch, but do not touch.
My skin traces air
does not separate me from the universe.

When I dance, I know her, my temptress.
I learned her from imitation—
practice, rehearsal.

I embody the best choreography
through cheers and screams,
the *Gorgeous* from my sensei.

We assume our skin
and must be taught
its power.

I was in siren school for many years
before they allowed me up on deck.
Now, I teach the acolytes.

Let me list the things I know —
I crave the power of the climb.
I devour rhythm and silk.
I am resilient.
The confidant woman has the strongest pull.

I fit inside my self.
My skin is not a boundary of texture.
My skin connects.

Here, on the ship, we are safe.
Out there, they take away
breasts
clitoris
hair
They cover skin, even eyes.
Our lure, too strong.

My canals are dry. Tight.
Never having birthed,
Never having owned another human.

But my rhythm silk skin
is permeable membrane connecting pleasure
to ocean
to air
and if I can be brave,
to other skin.

39

LIKE ALL THE REST

BY LINDA PRITCHER

Spittle face slob. Hard lover. Why did you do it? You dumb shit. So dumb you can't wipe your face of shame. You sweat where you lie, deep, where you think you can't be found out. But you can and you will. Hell is too good for you.

You smacked my bottom with your crusty square dance hands that day. They were red and oozing and puckered by shame. You tried to stick them to me, stick your shame on me.

Bottoms up you bastard. Where are you now, in prison? Were you there by 18? Did you lie with some girl at 16? Did she break you, break your heart, break you at your own game? She'd be so much better than you.

I turned to you on those stairs then. I didn't hide the tears. But I told. I told my momma on you. My momma spoke for me. She wouldn't leave me in your festering pile of shame and hurt. She knew that shame. She knew that hurt. She saw your imprint big as that ugly hand of yours under my skirt. That red-edged welt you left, was etched on my bottom like the bumps on your cracked and oozing skin, Gus. Yeah, Gus, that was your name. Did you hate your name? With all that dry, cracked, gussy-oozing skin over your arms, did you hate being you? Did you want to imprint your pain on me? Was there no one to speak up for you, bastard?

Well, it's too late for you and all your kind. That welt left defiance. You can't tame it, you can't stop it, you can't heal those wounds. There's no escape. My loathing knows no bounds. You're a faceless boy among boys, without number or name now. You're like all the rest in your great expectations. I don't care who you are. You'll do. You'll do for now. You're mine. You're mine for now. You're mine for the taking. Until I'm done with you, poor spittle faced slob, you're bound by my shameless laws.

40

LIFE'S MIRRORS

BY ANNA SCOTT

I feel the tension in my shoulders. I look up and see the crystal vase filled with the first cut roses. The buds are tight like my shoulders and their stems extend out of the vase and brag to the world of their beauty.

One stem cannot support the bud. It's too heavy, like the weight of a dead child buried years before. Another bud is sprightly, a young girl showing off new dance moves to her parents.

The flowers' apricot colors change as the evening sun bounces around the room. One moment a deep orange and the next a coral shimmer in the sea. The green leaves remind me of the divine masculine, standing present to the beauty of the feminine buds. Proud, supportive, and mesmerised by their beauty.

It's a waste to have these flowers in a vase. These roses need to be wild. Move with the wind. Provide a sweet smell to attract those who want to suck its beauty.

I planted each rose bush. We have gone through the seasons of life together. I care for them and they care for me. I buried my daughter's guinea pig in their soil. They produce flowers for me to relish in my dining room.

I prune them; I feed them with food better than most people

get to eat. I water them and sing them love songs and gape at their beauty. As the men do to me.

When they are pruned to their core, we have moments of silence, of loss. I know loss. I lost my husband. He lost his memory. We lost the family and life we dreamed of. They lost their buds; they lost their limbs.

We stare at each other. We know what life is like. Know that time will heal. From the depths of their despair, a new life will emerge and it will be beautiful. There will be colors I could not imagine. And there will be tragedy. Aphids, rust, or black spots. I will do my best to tend to this precious creature, but sometimes life has its own plans, no matter how much I care.

41

ALL'S FAIR IN LOVE AND WAR
BY DEL ADEY-JONES

I am not your sister. There is no hood here. There is no loyalty. There is no empathy. No compassion, no respect, no regard, no putting myself in your shoes. All's fair in love and war. Lock your husbands away. I'm coming for them. Don't judge them, me, or yourself. We are all complicit in this game.

I am hungry for power and control. I will covet what's not mine. I will use anything and everything at my disposal to feed my desire to conquer and win. I will coax and manipulate my way through life. I am hard as stone. Impenetrable to touch or emotion. Cold as ice on a burning hot summer's day.

I will seduce, charm, and cajole my way into every husband's vacuous hearts. I will entice them with lies and deception. I will fawn, flatter, and bolster their fragile egos. I will pump them up to then feast on their remains.

I will dance to their every perverted whim. I will bump and grind and whisper sounds of ecstasy into their ears. I've sold my soul to the devil. I will sink to the bowels of earth to fool them… subjugate myself to lure them into my beguiling web. I will feign affection until a more amusing diversion piques my curiosity. It's the thrill of the game. A cat toying with a mouse. Claws piercing skin. Blood oozing from fatal wounds.

Like a satiated vampire, my thirst for blood is quenched... for now. But soon the sweet taste of victory will fade, and the hunger and emptiness will return to gnaw away at my innards. The pain is unbearable. My only salve the promise of my next conquest.

I am dead. An empty vessel. A bottom less pit of neediness. A vacuous hole of nothingness. A receptacle for the dregs of life. I am devoid of honor, no moral high ground, no righteous indignation. I live in the squaller of despair and degradation. Used up, spent up, washed up, and hung out to dry. No heart, no soul, no self.

EPILOGUE - SIREN/SEDUCER/WHORE

Webster's definitions:
Siren, a temptress or a group of female and partly human crea-
tures in Greek mythology that lured mariners to destruction by
their singing.
Seducer, to persuade to disobedience or disloyalty, to lead astray,
to entice sexual intercourse.
Whore, a person who engages in sexual intercourse for pay.

This is always an interesting one for the student, and often what
is written has some sexual undercurrent. As humans, we don't
talk that much about sex, let alone write about it, so given the
opportunity to do so, you will see the writers have much to
share. And again, the writing isn't literal.

We all have a little bit of a siren in us, a bit of a seducer, a bit
of a whore. But what does that look like from an energetic
perspective? Where does your Whore energy live in your body,
and does it feel different from the energy of the Siren or Seducer?
There are subtle differences between them. Ponder that for a
moment and observe your own distinctions.

The surprise of the Muse exercise is that we just don't know
what is going to show up on the page, because we haven't

written from these energies before. Let's say you're writing a poem from the Seducer muse, but the writing is about running through the forest like a huntress. Perhaps for that writer the energy of their Seducer sounds like the Huntress muse to a reader. We don't know because the energy of the muses is individual.

> Curriculum directive: *This is not about knowing the various archetypes, about finding all you can online and reading about them. You might do a little research, but this is about finding the muse inside. Look past the word, past societal influence, past your judgement or opinion to the energy inside you.*

You have to be open to the energetic state of the muses. Some of the energy might be frenetic, some might be calm, weird, tired, or resigned and all of it will impact the words you use on the page.

Now, to look at a few pieces in this chapter. In Vanessa's piece, "On The Ship," she writes: *My canals are dry. Tight. Never having birthed.* She could be writing from the Mother muse. But the references to *silk skin and permeable membranes connecting pleasure* offer a different undertone. Read it out loud and listen to the energy and beat of the writing.

I love in Maria's piece, "Loves Original Promise," how there is a juxtaposition to this poem. Part 1 is beautiful and expansive and then boom! *I weep for the soul that flounders...* Right there's the complexity of the human relationship with self, muse regardless. And then Sharon's piece, "Gravity," that last line, *A never-gone breathes me out as my hips lift to his gaze.*

Jules Swales

PART V

MUSE FIVE

42

FUEL OF PAIN

BY ANNA SCOTT

I quiet my breath. I have learned how to be silent. I have learned how to roll, with little dust kicked up. I am a leaf that falls to the ground, swaying with the wind.

I love being this way. It wasn't easy getting here.

I am patient. I know not to hurry. I wait for things to rise in their own time, like bread. I wait for things to age to precision, like a fine wine in an oak barrel.

The first thing I learned was how to close my heart.

I notice the small branch broken on the ground, the painting that is moved a smidge, the shirt untucked. I notice the consistent number of veins in each blue hydrangea leaf, the handle of the coffee pot in a different position. Your breath change when I approach.

My mother taught me this when I was seven years old. I learned how to go against my nature to do this.

I am fast. I have a daily practice of lunging from a starting block. I can move from stillness to jet speed. I don't need to warm up. I am a thoroughbred in a human body.

My mother taught me this because she was dying, and she wanted me to survive on my own. She knew if I didn't have her energy, my survival system would kick in. The pain of being closed off was the fuel I needed to learn and grow.

I am precise. Every movement is intended. I am an elegant ballerina in a Balanchine ballet. No extra steps. My arms move to their positions as I leap through the air and land in the intended spot. I know the exact place to break an animal's neck for the fastest death.

I move mountains to not feel pain. I didn't see the gift of pain. Pain is the enemy.

I have perfect timing. I can sense the space open up and I move into it. I sense when you are getting close and I show up right in front of you. I see you think that you are going to beat me this time. But you won't.

I thought my mother was a cold-hearted bitch who was disconnected from her children. I learned that I should be the same. Now I see we are never disconnected.

43

ESSENCE

BY AL MILLEDGE

The wind blows my mind. There's part of me that hides in shadows. I won't tell it, or you will think of me every time it slips across your horizon. I'll only be the clipped in, filmed over, pinned up state of my forever changed biology.

I refuse to be what proliferates inside me. I'm mutated by drugs, a biological alien, cells capped off, sentries released from the belvedere at the slightest whiff of a blood vessel on the morph. I am everyone's biology. I am a statement of what it is to show up as human right now. I am the thrill of balance lost in an overthrow of limbs and giggles. I'm not a government department or a keyboard shortcut. I won't be labelled by an acronym.

My poor Jewish Grandma, the life source of our family, saw my femininity peek out, back when I didn't know to hide it. She trained me on how women of her time and status got through life, so that I understood, I had choices. She taught me to outsmart the privileged and use the width of my shoulders. She was smart in a way that I had no idea was smart. She's the reason I'm still here. The reason I pick myself up. The reason I didn't fall on the hedonist's battlefield, where I was an eager soldier in skirmish after skirmish.

I wish I had met the woman who had taught her, a warrior.

She would have been layers of thin steel and delicate bruised blue flesh. All the abuse, bullwork and gritted silence concentrated in a single sticky drop and passed through the vessel of motherhood into me. This tough woman's way has been thought of as a curse in our family. An ill-humoured bitter cynicism that made up the meat of our legacy, but we were looking at it arseways in the mirror. It was pure. It was my survival. Survival of angry contact, survival of misplaced trust, survival of dark alleys and the celebration of hate out in the full glare of daylight. Survival of love and friendship lost.

When I caved into self-loathing, I allowed the rescue, allowed the tubes and the donations and the love. Became a survivor. Her essence is my drug of choice. The daily pills I swallow are to remind my biology, her biology, it's bulletproof.

44

MY KINGDOM WILL COME

BY MER MONSON

The pain is loud in the waking quiet. I lie still under the covers, watching her crawl into my neck and shoulders and down into my hips. She spreads her shiny hard wings, gearing up for a full day's ride. I breathe and lick my wounds. I am hungry, hungry to leave the castle, hungry for my kingdom.

I cannot untangle the hunger from the hurt. They are both obstinate. They both beat through my body like a drum. They both call me out beyond the domesticated woman I have become and into the wild. I try to bury them, quiet them, ignore them, heal them or feed them to the wolves, but they will not let go. My kingdom calls to me. It is not in this house, in this aching body, or in this bed.

When moonlight comes, I wander, cradled in a woolen blanket and bare feet. My body weeps, as there are no more reasons to muzzle my discontent. I meet her, the medicine woman. We sit on the cool earth. She holds my wet face in her gnarled hands and fills my pockets of ache with moonlight. My cramped up lungs breathe. Her obsidian eyes whisper to me. The pain will quiet. The hunger will be fed. You will find what you hunt, far, far away and in this castle of blood and bone. We sit in silence as moon dust sifts down through my skin and lights the next step in front of me.

I move in the light. I follow the drumbeat. I run with the wolves. I move through the pain and because of the pain. I am steeped in the knowing of what calls to me, a siren in my heart that floods the rest of me with juice and muscle.

And when the pain overtakes, I stop. I rest with this dragon, the one only I can see and feel beneath my skin. I lay down my sword, open my lonely eyes and drink her in. I touch her hard, wet scales and breathe in her aches of smoke and flame. I curl up beside her and let her troubled anger stretch wide in the arms of what shelters us both in the wind. I can hear the wind. It's whispering to me. My kingdom will come, my kingdom will come, my kingdom will come.

45

THE WOMAN NO ONE TAUGHT ME HOW TO BE

BY JENNIE LINTHORST

Watch me closely, and you will see a level of hyper-vigilance. I turn on my inner clock to never be late for an appointment, research the best therapist for my son, double-check the math of our budget. My training ground for fear runs from 3 to 5 a.m. — scripts are written, muscles sculpted, swords drawn for imagined battles ahead. I stand on a mountaintop of pride when the week's meals are planned, and each ingredient is tucked away in my refrigerator. I'm not crazy. I've just been awake and watching like a lynx who only comes out at night, watching for weakness, watching for lessons on how to survive, watching for how to be this woman no one taught me how to be. The emotional scar tissue left from my mother's young death still speaks to me, says, *I can't; I can't sit with this rawness; I can't navigate this thing called life.* So, I learned to watch and listen, fill my arsenal of protection from stories of women who came before me. I map their battles, their triumphs, collect their keys to healthy love. I am vigilant against danger that encroaches upon anyone. Loyalty is my religion. I will limp the extra mile to show you to the other side, carry your load, and unpack it with you, lesson by lesson learned. Sacred are the few in my life who know how to lead me to safer pastures, know how to coax me to take off my armor for a stretch, know how to stir my joy, release fits of laughter, walk with me into bursts of spontaneous sunshine. They know that it is here that I can rest. It is here that I can sleep the restorative sleep. Here, I can begin to face tomorrow's shadow.

46

FAITH. FULL STOP
BY MARIA ILIFFE-WOOD

There's a rumble in my tumble and I've let that feeling fool me in the past. Fool me into submission. Fool me into caving in. Fool me into giving up at the first hurdle. Fool me into losing myself and my faith along with it.

Faith. The eternal go-getter. The thing that keeps me going when all else fails. The invisible variable that determines whether I stay put or go for it. The feeling I tossed aside all those years ago when I thought God had forsaken me. The anchor that keeps my feet on the ground and my pen on the page.

Faith. The knowing that everything will be ok, no matter how it turns out. That harbinger of everything good in my life, when I thought I was in control of my destiny. The feeling in my belly that says 'You got this' when every other part of my body is screaming at me to halt.

Faith. The determination that has such quiet assurance. It brooks no argument and countenances no doubt.

It comes from a deep place. I know it doesn't come from me. It exists in spite of my limitations and frailties. It exists alongside hope and love, those other two commodities that seem like they are in short supply. It exists despite the world's insistence that it shouldn't.

It exists in me, and because it exists, I exist.
Faith has been the saving grace of my whole life.
Not faith in something.
Not faith in myself.
Not faith in God.
Just Faith… Full stop.

47

ALONE

BY LN SHEFFIELD

It's a blustery old day. The wind howling like crazy. I'm uptight. I'm tense. My whole body is on my guard.

No trust in life or my good old pen. A thousand steps back. The one who takes it all on my shoulders. Life is a burden. A heavy one to bear. I match the outside weather. I'm irritable and crave the chance to run outside and howl like the wind. Let it all out. This anger and restlessness wants to be set free. My world caves in on me.

A need in me to wrap up and protect this innocence. This Lu who has been cracked wide open. I'm retreating back in. My instincts tell me, be kind. Harden up. Protect. This soft exterior has taken enough. I need to be on high alert. Not allow the trampling of others.

I am a vessel to the unknown. I give too much.

I have a deep urge to explode. To claw at the raw earth. To feel the soil in my fingernails. To scream loud and release this inner beast of wildness into nature. I crave the chance to dance in the wind with the trees. To allow my whole body to flop. To allow the earth to swallow me. To allow those deep routed pains to leave me.

In all my glory, I wish to be naked and run through the

woods, as the animals in the forest follow my path. They too run with me, dance with me, scream with me, claw the earth with me, swim in the lakes with me. I am a caged animal. A child of the earth. A wild being ready to be let loose. Be seen and heard, yet with the shackles intact. The protection around me.

Nature holds me, as my throat opens wide to the wails and screams that threaten to over spill. An over bearing energy grounds me and lifts me at the same time. I rise like a phoenix from the ashes. My senses leave.

I fold into the earth. A groundedness like no other. I sink deep onto my knees and cradle that which is before me. My dagger that protects me. It dissolves before my very eyes.

I am left - alone.

48

THIS IS IT

BY N. VYAS

I believe in the mystical,
then I forget.
Pierce through the veil.
Destroy the mess layered on top —

layers and layers of story and doubt.
For a brief respite, all was wiped away.
I could see. I remembered,
not just darkness, but possibility.

I will myself to go through the portal,
to stop hiding, to let grief ravage me.
I'm not afraid of you, I say,
have your way with me.

Let my heart be blasted with anguish,
let sorrow drown my breath.
Let me sip you in, exhale you out,
swim in your essence,

become the element in which I reside.
I'm done with my battle against you,
done with the pretense of your nonexistence,
done with the notion that you

pass through me like clouds.
The truth of you is as deep as the Universe is vast.
Why then do I live in your shallow waters,
and think I've tasted enough for one lifetime?

Because I'm afraid your ancient power
will crush me into dust.
This is not surrender.
This is the beginning of beginnings.

49

BLOOD

BY SAMANTHA HERMAN

I had to pull down brave from wherever it had been hiding. I sat back in the cold car and focused on the dark shapes scurrying in and out of the council block. The reptilian part of my brain focused on satisfaction, my hands methodically binding wire into makeshift handcuffs. An eye for an eye that was clean. I didn't want clean. I wanted to see him fucking scream as I took a baseball bat to his testicles. That kept my blood pumping.

The day before, I only had to wait thirty patient minutes before PC Plod clocked off and I slipped under the flimsy police cordon into that familiar hallway.

Truth is, I don't know how I did it. I died a thousand deaths those first few hours. Every sound threatened a noose around my neck, every creak a razor to my throat, every shadow a hammer to my skull. Stifling tears, I began the metamorphosis into the other, the bloodhound me festering in my DNA. I had to force it into being.

I pounded my feet down the hallway and near barrelled into the bedroom. A tornado of pain slapped my face as I caught her scent lingering in scattered clothes and damp towels. I rummaged through twisted bed sheets, bile rising as I spotted dried come stains. It was worth it. I came up with the big break, a half-twisted photo, you know the old-fashioned kind, an actual piece of paper. It was lodged just under the mattress. He had taken her phone, probably thinking that would eliminate any visuals, but ha, fucker, I got ya. I whooped my arm into the empty room. The document shredder was full and buzzing. It had been used recently. Shredded papers gave me the other clues I needed. He thought I would play by the rules. Cunt. What an absolute narcissistic tosser of colossal proportions, not thinking I could or would figure it out.

So that was why I came to be sitting in the clapped out hire car outside the dingiest council block on the coldest fucking night Glasgow had to offer. I was on the trail. I had his scent in my sights. I had slowed my breath, not wanting to fog up the windscreen, but hey who needs oxygen when the game is so close by.

He was going to pass within a whisper of me and not have the faintest. I had hammered nails in the bat, secured the Stanley knife in my right-hand pocket; a scalpel was taped to my left ankle. Game on.

50

WELL DONE

BY VANESSA POSTER

She is muscle, my huntress, so well done, there is no juice when you press. She is leather wrapped flesh, hidden behind the noise of wind on aluminum foil, the tap of blinds against string, the hint of music from teenagers rehearsing in the football field.

She has slept in my abdominal wall holding nakedness to softened bones. She craves silence to hear the jet trail, humming-bird wings, and running feet in rotted leaves.

The truth at her core is vulnerability and a hunger for savage danger and betrayal.

In attack, her adrenaline kicks in, lifts me off the path as the viper's fangs slither. But personal betrayal, the drip of poison into a friendship, takes time for the venom to absorb, the dye fade, the water clear. She can't save me from betrayal. I know this, and still wish for her to grasp my arms, lift me, open me.

I deceived and imprisoned her in this muscle when I was seven years old.

"Come back at 3:15," the nice lady, with short white hair, had said.

We were in an office where children did not come unless summoned. A stack of papers and a number 2 pencil placed on a round table with two adult-sized chairs.

"How will I know when it's 3:15?" I asked. The lady wore a pale blue jacket, white blouse, matching skirt, and sensible shoes to conduct the IQ test that labeled me *gifted*.

"Here," the lady said, and pulled open an accordion gold band and hung it loose over my young wrist. The watch face a shimmering abalone, with inlaid Roman numerals.

"When the small and the large hand are both here," she said, pointing to the three capital letter i's.

In the playground, I did not clear the bases or climb the jungle gym. I did not make a fist to sock the red pock-marked rubber ball. I would be mortified to break or lose this precious bit of gold and shell.

It was the day I chose my nature as *good* girl, immersed my huntress power in muscle, hid her, betrayed her.

It wasn't the IQ test that told me I was special. It was the lady's faith to hand me such a beautiful thing and to know I would keep it safe from danger and return with it at the precise, pre-appointed time.

51

COCKTAIL OF DESIRE

BY JB HOLLOWS

The urge stirs deep inside my belly. It uncoils with fierce breath. It ignites my dormant spark. It skulks deep in the recesses of my body. I try to flush it out. Tempt it like I would a cat. Offer treats, encouragement, sacrifice. It doesn't care. It knows my tricks. It sees through my tease.

You can't outwit wit.

I see a flicker of movement. I feel my muscles in spontaneous flex. My mouth salivates.

I lick my lips with my salacious, fat tongue. Desire droops my eyelids. My hand slides down my belly. Too soon. Way too soon. The moist dew on my red lips shows my card too soon, and she hides again. A silent retreat into the folds of my sanctum. My veins settle. My blood cools.

It's not shy. Oh no, that's not it. It would be easy to think that. Obvious even. But that's not it at all.

It's not bored. It's too patient to be bored. It can lie there for months, years, decades even. It waits until: The time is right. The moon is full. The stars are aligned. The moment is ripe.

It waits until the yearn is too strong to resist.

I wait. My breath does not shift a wisp of air.

I wait.

I wait until I feel that twitch again. Hunger spreads my limbs of their own accord. Muscles ripple, luxuriate, stretch.

Hairs raise up to capture the mood, to feel the air brush its follicles, to prepare the body to pounce. Tastebuds uncurl, ready for the feast to come.

Groin aches with want. Thighs tighten for the ride. Toes curl in anticipation of the earth warm beneath my feet. The smell of fear and fur, sweat and piss, newborn and victory, drive the destruction to come.

The taste of surrender intoxicates my blood with a cocktail of desire.

EPILOGUE - HUNTRESS/HUNTER

Webster's definition: a woman who hunts, or a person or animal who hunts.

When I first did the Huntress muse exercise, I imagined her being fierce, dressed in animal pelts, and galloping through the forest on a black stallion. Yes, I went totally literal, and that was quite fun. Then I started to look beneath the fierce woman on the horse to the spirit. I was surprised to find the energy was stifled and mute. She felt gagged and stripped of power. She wasn't just exhausted; she was silenced.

When I connected to the energy of this internal silence, it impacted my writing. My sentences became clipped, short, staccato, like I was gasping for air. The deep, energetic state affected the whole nature of my voice, language, the prosody of the line itself.

> Curriculum directive: *You must be open to a surprise, be willing to write something unexpected, be open to the exercise. And remember, do not write a piece and then decide after what the muse is. To get the most impact from the Muse exercise, you must forget all those great stories you want to share and just do the exercise.*

There is such diversity in these Huntress/Hunter pieces. JB's piece, "Cocktail of Desire," is an invitation to look for our own urge, stirring deep inside. Can you see the breathlessness of the short sentences? In Anna's piece, "Fuel of Pain," there is the subtle quashing of the human spirit throughout: *I had to learn how to go against my nature.*

In Sam's piece, "Blood," wow, ok, so the pulse of the hunter is raw and alive. Almost like the writer was given permission, through the exercise, to find the energy and the words inside. *Game on.*

> Curriculum directive: *Settle into your body. Settle into your history, this lifetime and others. Settle into the cry, the laughter, the gurgle, the prayer, the promise, and the wisdom of your muse energy. Settle in to a new landscape inside and write from there.*

If you are going to explore the Muse exercise for yourself, a great tip to help loosen up the energy is to move around a bit. Shake your body. Have some fun with it. Test yourself and enjoy the challenge of meeting yourself on the page in a new way. So much of our life is either habit or routine; challenge yourself a bit and pilgrim your writing into a new landscape.

Jack Grapes: *The purpose of this exercise is not to get it right, since energy states are subjective.*

Or to quote Mary Oliver: *You do not have to be good. You do not have to walk on your knees for a hundred miles through the desert repenting. You only have to let the soft animal of your body love what it loves.*

Jules Swales

PART VI

MUSE SIX

I AM THE FIRE

BY SHARON STRIMLING

Fire licks at my skin,
my upper lip,
the sides of my temples,
the space between my eyes.

I scan the room for black holes
to turn time,
and swallow screams.
There are none.

Just living flames, born of lies.
In the hot pools of my sex,
beneath the force of my love,
under the devotion of my heart,

You lied.
You lied as you stoked my fire,
and lied
as it warmed your skin.

And when by the chill of your lies,
you shivered, drew cold,
you lied more, and stoked more,
your bellow's kiss pulling embers,

with the sea at your back
and your lover behind you,
hoping, stroking, waiting,
she braced your raft.

And now, cool and safe,
you've found the open sea
where the storms of lies don't crash.
Tell the truth, I said. But you didn't.

So, I turned to her,
your precious and pretend Athena,
your goddess of the Not True, the Veiled,
the Sacred, Perverted.

I screamed to her of the broken sisterhood,
the faded sacrifice of Avalon,
the mists that blew
and left it naked.

Tell the truth, I said. But she didn't.
She, who pawned truth for your skin,
then powdered her nose
with my ashes.

I swallowed your lies
like an earthquake swallows
a sweltered city.
They burned my core molten,

rumbled my dreams,
boiled my joints,
blistered my nails,
bulged my eyes.

And I kept still —
let the world sleep
lulled by fake gods
and false goddesses.

Now the rumbles are louder,
the wind's stolen the flames
and I burn.
I am the fire.

I am the fire that began
before the blaming of Eve.
That folded itself around
all the rapes of all the wars.

That dragged the third wife
and fourth wife
and fifth wife
to guillotine.

I am the fire
that burned tiny souls, soles first
with felled trees
from aching forests.

I am the fire
that bound girls to chains and whips,
to gagged jaws and tongues rolled out,
glued to shut doors of libraries and law.

I am the fire
that began before the fear of itself,
and reminders of its empty Nothing,
quivered bodies on the ash wings of death.

I am the fire
that began before the blaming of Eve
when sister turned on sister
and the silence of man lay still.

53

DON'T CROSS ME

BY LINDA SANDEL PETTIT

"Why did you write, 'don't cross me' in your essay about the Divine Feminine?" a male reader said. "Why were you so pugilistic?"

Pugilistic? That has something to do with boxing, right? Taking a fighter's stance? Let me tell you, there are more than a few males I could swing at. I won't pull punches.

My first boyfriend. At age 15, the car door handle tattooed a crater into my upper back as I struggled to heave him off. My scared sobs might have interrupted a rape. I'd paralyze him in a headlock and clean his clock if I could.

My boss. He pushed me against a wall, grabbed my breasts and shoved his tongue in my mouth. I squeaked out a "please, no" against the strangle of a foreign tongue. He begged my quiet. He said he had mis-read my "signals"—my friendliness. His transgression was my fault. He was black; my complaint would have cost him his job. I liked him; I gave him the benefit of the doubt and didn't breathe a word. He deserved a swift kick in the nuts.

A fellow writer. He showed up at my dorm room drunk. I had a crush on him, and we made out. I said I didn't want to go all the way—I was a virgin. He flipped like a whale and locked me into a 69 position. I was pinioned to the bed by his weight. His penis, like a giant stiff worm with a mushroom head, hung over me.

I'd never seen a dick so up close and personal. It stank of urine. I fought a crazy urge to bite it. With herculean effort rooted in panic, I pushed him off and out the door. I cried as he swore at me. I was a "dick teaser." From my sixth-floor window, I watched him tear out of the parking lot. The wheels on his GTO coughed smoke as entitled anger laid rubber on the cement. I shook like a leaf.

My first fiancé. I caught him in flagrante delicto with another woman. His betrayal plunged me into a black hole of grief that swallowed a year of my life.

Degradation. Humiliation. Shame. Betrayal. Anger. Mansplaining. Bropropriating. Manterrupting. I've had it. *I'm no misandrist.* For every man who has treated me like dirt, there have been two or three who've helped me get a leg up in life. But the dirt pile suffocates. Like so many sisters, I'm digging out from under the manure of male privilege. Enough is enough. So no, don't cross me.

54

THE LIE OF DOMESTICATION
BY JB HOLLOWS

I'm drained. I'm tired. I need sleep. The sleep of babies. The kind of sleep that softens life. Removes. Transports. Deletes. Where I don't have to try. Where nothing goes wrong. Where there is no right.

That world where I can drop my mask. Let go my shield. Release my demons. Forgo my desires. Free my expectations.

Where I'm not wanted, needed, demanded, in charge, charged up.

Where it's okay to stop. Pause. Rest.

Where my eyes no longer gaze. No sight. No flight. No right.

Or Wrong.

I'm desperate, drained, dreary. I fall with boring regularity into an abyss of failure. I fret about the harm I've caused. The unexpected pain. The accidental destruction.

Of all I love.

Can I love anything that's not me? Is it a lie, a false declaration of dependence? Because only I can see what is to be seen. Only I see me. In my full glory and in my darkest despair. Only I see what lies beneath. Beneath the lies. Beneath the hopes. Beneath the thin veneer of domestication.

My worry is not that I'm weak, pathetic, irrelevant. My fear is that the power unleashed will destroy what I've come to rely on, the normality, the mundane, the benign. That which keeps me from this ridiculous notion that I matter.

My concern is that once my strength ravages the made-up castles of sand and sundown's, they can never be rebuilt.

I drape my body with guilty pleasures to hide its wanton desire to have it all.

I fix my smile with the pale powder of normal and the red paint of sex to hide the gnashing fangs of hunger.

I swamp my mind with endless lists of things to be done, to hide my pulsating longing to not do anything.

Contained, corralled, curtailed. My life is a long tail of dutiful deliverance. Of never quite living up to the hype of bending in so many directions. I'm a chiropractor's dream.

Sleep frees me from the chains of being tamed.

Provides a space where the energy surge has no discernible effect. Allows the dice to fall where they may without my interminable interference.

With the end of every sleep, I perform the empty daily ritual.

I dress in layers of civilised bliss.

I eat a hearty breakfast of rules sprinkled with empty promises.

I face the world with the acceptable half of me that's wearing thin.

And with each day, I flag with the effort of squeezing my oversized ego into my over polished carcass.

55

TORN

BY AL MILLEDGE

I trample all over my past. I poke around to find the thought that palpitates loudest and then sit and splash in its ugly beauty, until I feel pain sear through each of the valves that pump life to my core. My chest cramps. Long, cold tentacles probe under my ribs. They suffocate and tug me down. They hold me in place. No breath. I wait for anything else. I wait for it to finish. I wait for night to fall.

It doesn't come.

I gouge into the long-closed wounds of past relationships. Dig in sharp and deep and gnaw through thick scar tissue. Spend hours checking every gristly permutation, every ugly word, every wisp of meaning. I rummage around in all the '*but, they said's*' that I can clasp fingers of memory onto and flick them to and fro until I find the righteous blame that I am looking for.

It doesn't come.

I outlived the tight band of brothers and lovers. We stood on the back of bunting covered trucks together. We danced and kissed and hugged and fucked. Demetri, who used to ride his poxy horse up and down the Euston Rd, waved his fist and shouted in angry Greek at any driver who got too close. Russel, a beautiful clippie on the old-style buses who made a joke of everything, along with my love for him. Harry, the sweetest east end villain I ever met. I hanker after the fraternity, the union.

It doesn't come.

The romantic love I think I want now, the touch I crave, the checklist of needs to be ticked. The homestead of wrangled emotions that have to be in place before I'll be content. My fervent lack of commitment to anyone who shows an interest. My smear of disregard for those who don't measure up. My foot against the jam to anyone who tries to push the door into my life open more than a crack. One wrong word and I'm done. Door shut, curtain closed, vent open to clear the smog. I don't need their love.

It doesn't come.

56

THE TRUTH IN ME

BY ANNA SCOTT

I don't want to write.

It is like a letter from the IRS and I refuse to open it. It stares at me. I am afraid of what it will say and its consequences.

I have a fruit pit in my stomach and something growing in me. I have no idea what it is.

I don't know who I am when I write. I am taken over by some being that uses me to move my fingers and type its secret message to the world. My breath shortens and tears fill my eyes. I lose control of my identity.

This energy is creepy, wild and extreme. One moment I dance with erotic pleasure and the next I take a needle out of my hair and stab my dance partner. I use the dripping blood to paint a beautiful portrait of my daughter or a surrealist masterpiece.

This energy has no bounds. It is a complete free-fall with no parachute. Everything I have ever known is being deleted. This kind person, who I have made myself to be, is obliviated, like an egg thrown to the ground. Nothing is left of me but little shattered sticky pieces. Instead, comes in a being that is willing to do anything. It has no shame or fear. It knows its power. It has fun playing, while it watches me squirm and tighten my vagina as I witness.

I am not this energy. It is someone else. I am too afraid to admit that I am this, and so much more. My kindness has been my jail.

My boyfriend has always seen the truth in me. He says he won't mess with me because I will go straight for the jugular. Cut his balls off.

He is right. When I write, I will. And part of me will love it. Part of me will relish what it is to make a clean slice. Part of me will open his mouth and place them, oh so gently, in his gaping mouth while I watch his eyes bulge out.

57

TIME IS DEAD

BY N. VYAS

Tick. Tock. Time is dead.
My heartbeat slows.
I'm locked in a land of

no th i n g n e s s.
A sandstorm descends.
In its grip, grimy particles

of earth swirl
into my mouth, my eyes, my bones.
No sign of life,

the empty sky turns to ash.
No horizon, a singular haze.
No time, I'm lost again.

I would cry if I could,
but tear ducts remain
barren as the land.

My body ravaged,
yet, I cling to myself.
I drag this body on elbows, knees,

to find life,
some semblance of me.
A drop will do.

Tick. Tock.
Dark night will be my salve.
Moonlight, my balm.

There are no decisions left, I am —
like time, sky, earth, or rain.
Death lingers at the periphery, at the edge beyond now.

I see Him, but there's no fight to be had.
I who once fought for a living,
admit, it was all for naught.

Tick—there is no past.
Tock—there is no future.
The sun sets. I'm still here.

58

BIG TALK

BY MARIA ILIFFE-WOOD

If I had a stitch in time, I'd be doing fine, you know what I mean. God's little apples make a merry cider before they rot to high heaven and go back to whence they came. I'll take one last clutch at life, thank you very much.

I want to squeeze every last drop out of this dance. I'm going to quickstep as long as I can, before the last waltz slows me down. Even if it means I have to run the gauntlet and ram down doors at full pelt. I'm here to live life, not sit in the doldrums and whine 'poor me'.

I can shout loud and proud, sat here in the comfort of my dressing gown. I write a good story, maybe even convince myself that I'm something special, that I'm going places. Yeah! I'm full of that shit.

I try to prove myself to the unknown and unseen. Talk to myself because no one else will listen and for good reason. Who wants to hear the crap I tell myself? I wouldn't spew it on my worst enemy. And if you believe that, you'll believe anything. If I could get out from under this dungheap, I'd sure as hell hand it over to someone else to carry for me.

I know! I talk big for a little 'un! I whack up the volume of my own glorification, ruffle my wing feathers and fly up to a heady height, so I can look down my nose at all and sundry. Do I feel better for it? You bet your bottom dollar I do. For a nanosecond.

Then my house of cards tumbles down and I take a long hard look in the mirror and realise we're the same you and I.

And that's a blessing, not a curse.

59

THE FISH HATCHERY

BY VANESSA POSTER

I throw a handful of dry feed into the pool of fish.
Trout swarm and hunger
sleek and silver boiling, a stew of writhing fish,
oil jigging in the bottom of a pan.

My heart jigging in the bottom of a pan.
Heartbreak, like death, not a sudden grapple
of worm on a line, but a drawn-out building of a dam,
stick by stick.

My best friend broke my heart.
This woman who held me up.
This woman who helped me calm Morgan's dragons as he
    died.
This woman who showed me cinderblocks under the
    house where she grew up.

My grief over Morgan's death killed our friendship.
I asked for just one word of truth from her,
tying a line to her deepest core,
pulling it through with barbs.

Please, just one word of truth, but no.
It had to be a whole story about umbrellas.
Juggling all the umbrellas for everyone.
Needing to hold her own umbrella, not mine.

I was already holding my own umbrella.
Didn't need her to hold one for me.
She is gone. Done with me.

The dry feed rains down.
I sizzle and boil.

60

THE DEMONS WILL FALL

BY MER MONSON

I have to dig deep for this woman to show her face. I lay the shovel down and look in her eyes. She reeks something awful, her hair a raven's nest. I lock my stomach, a reflex I can't unstitch from my story, but something pulls me in. I know those icy blue eyes, that clenched-in-stone jaw, that belly on fire. As we sit in silence, I can hear the rushing sound of my own fury.

I hear the smack of a tennis ball gunned with every nerve and muscle. I hear journal pages inked with hate, torn out, and trashed for shame. I hear teenage teeth grinding against the edge of my female place. I hear my gut crackle and hiss, the moment I know my sister's husband has been beating her for years. I hear the energy healer's words, "I see a long line of women behind you, women who'd rather get cancer than get angry." I hear my hands muzzle my own mouth, pleading with myself not to make waves.

Cancer comes, and with it the urge to wake up all my dead parts. I ask my love to get an old car door from the junkyard. "Why?" he says. "To beat the hell out of it," I say. I shatter glass and bang up metal until the door cracks open inside, until the hungry truth pushes its way up, until all of me can breathe. Wearing my rage on the outside is a damn relief. No more burying the blackness for safety, for belonging, for mother's milk. My body knows. Fury must be loved with arms wider than its own and let onto the dance floor, before it can weave its way to higher ground.

I smile now each time I step into her strong warm skin, into this long-cramped layer of my own. I look at her in the mirror, dazzling in the grandeur of fully grown woman flesh, wild hair flying like ravens. The earth's demons are swept up by a silent washing of their feet as I stand my ground, make space for holy eruption, and raise my arms until the vastness of the heart is cradled back to its throne. And as the demons fall, they will look and they will see — the child, the maiden, the mother, the huntress, the crone, the seductress and I — we are all the arms and breath of God.

61

HIDE AND SEEK, HATEFUL STYLE
BY LINDA PRITCHER

Walking seems so pedestrian, skipping so childlike. My raking claws clatter and scrape along the sidewalk, where friends color their chalk dreams into bright hieroglyphic pyramids. My dark streaks howl at their playfulness. I groan at their delight, their heads bowed over whispers, girly secrets, fireflies, cracker jacks and board games. Sly is their contempt for me, never chosen to play, shamed by exclusion. I hate their charms, their softness, their joy. I rumble with brittle-ridden rage at their days, at my rough longing, grating at their gates.

Shouting and dashing through the woods, didn't they see me behind every tree? Didn't they want to join in my new game? Didn't they want to play Hide and Seek, Hateful Style?

"Hi Charlotte," I said in my sweetest voice from behind a tree. "Remember me?"

The woods had grown quiet, the summer air turned cold. Charlotte was statue still. There, in her frilly embroidered bandana top and matching shorts dotted with colored chalk, she looked small and delicate. Beside her, Jill stood frozen. Her dark hair and single braid, tied off with a bright elastic band, lay resting on her bare shoulder. Stray strands of hair brushed up against the plastic bead chain she wore around her neck. A crushed acorn, its center laid bare, nestled beside her bright pink sneakers streaked with dirt. Backlit by the fading light, there was a soft ripeness to them. Such easy prey.

Charlotte's doll, held by a single arm, dangled at her side. Her left sandal had become unbuckled, revealing the origins of a deep red scratch that wound up her leg.

Hard to run, I thought.

The sallowness of the day retreated. Twilight smothered what was left. Dusky shades of descending plum swelled my desire for revenge.

They should have paid attention to the deep green conifers waving their arms in warning distress. They should have seen their fate. The woods were full of warnings. The woods had tried to protect them. Too busy with their stupid little games to notice. Too late.

"Who is there?" Charlotte murmured, eyes darting among the trees.

I struck with lightning speed. Wild blueberries shook from their branches. One swoop and it was over. A shriek of circling ravens muffled their cries.

My rage recedes as acorns bob on red rivulets. Midnight descends once again. I am cleansed. I am whole. I am avenged.

62

DANDELION

BY SAMANTHA HERMAN

Fury is my fuel now. A slow simmering never over the boil, precise level of energy, a dormant volcano lurking. But before, you must understand before. Before my skin was thick enough to contain me, I would slip out past the bounds of my body, cartwheeling away from sensation and sensitivity, a perfect line of spinning limbs as light and free as dandelion seeds. Bouncing off the ground, picking up speed and velocity, sun-kissed braids snapping around my ears and eyes, laughter escaping from my lungs.

I thought I roamed unnoticed. I was naïve, innocent, a lamb to the slaughter. The gods on high had a plan for me. They recognized my matchless sentiency as a tool they could activate. The very thing that made it impossible for me to feel free inside my skin, was the Achillean flaw they could twist and turn to some other more infamous use. I didn't recognize what was happening, so thirsty was I for affection and safety. A reverse osmosis adaptation of my genes, pushing, shaping and manipulating, until dandelion lightness was replaced with lead in my bones. My screams of despair ignored as my hair was shorn, ringlet by ringlet, braid by braid. It tumbled to the ground as my skin wrapped itself vice-like around my frame. Bare cheekbones winced in the cold wind, tears fell from my stony eyes for the last time. The truth of humanity was inescapable. A cesspit of sin. Arrogance, entitlement, disrespect, false grandeur, domination, cruelty, abuse, I felt it all. My blood, re-routed through dismay, sprung from my heart, ready for vengeance. Odium dictated my days. My nights were spent perfecting my skill, penance howling for satisfaction, my constant companion.

Year by year my hair returned, not as it once was, no that is forever lost. I now have thorns where once were ringlets. I have traitors attached to my skull. These familiars provoke and stir me, never allowing repose, a constant spiking of acid in my throat, a relentless need to decimate.

Whatever small shards of compassion were left were pulled one by one from the illusion of a heart. A time bomb sat in its place until all remembrances of cartwheels and laughter were crushed into a frenzy of bitterness and spite. That is how I came to being. I pass judgment. I excel in it, that is what keeps the fury at its constant action-ready roil.

Encased forever in this excruciating skin, I cleanse, edit, remove. I am judge and executioner. The decree is terminal.

EPILOGUE - MEDUSA

Webster's definition: a mortal Gorgon (a creature in Greek mythology) who is slain when decapitated by Perseus.

Medusa causes quite a stir for many students when they spend their writing week with her. Either the writer has no idea who Medusa is, and gets lost on Google, reading about her, or they think she is going to conjure up lots of rage-filled, army slaying writing. But again, and not to sound like a broken record, that would be too literal.

The Medusa muse can be a gorgeous journey for many. I cannot preempt what it might be for you, but often, Medusa enlivens a power point in the writer's body, which may have been dormant, one that will permeate each sentence they write. *In Method Writing we are always working on the voice, on tone, on rhythm, on diction, on how the energy of the piece of writing affects the reader.* — Jack Grapes

But I'm confused, you might be thinking. Well, don't be confused, that just implies you are trying to 'work it out.' Don't overcomplicate this. It's just a writing exercise that requires a connection with an energy, your Medusa energy. It's just you, writing about yourself, but you're doing it from the energy of Medusa.

> Curriculum directive: *This is not a therapeutic process. You're not doing a Gestalt exercise. This is writing. You pick a different muse each week and you write from the energy of that muse. It will be different from any other person's muse because it is coming from you and there is only one of you on the whole planet.*

When you read N.Vyas' piece, "Time is Dead," you will see how her Medusa muse was exhausted. This was a shock to her, as she was convinced it would be all fire and brimstone. But no. The Muse energy she reached was plain tired. Kudos to her for going with the energy and not trying to make the writing something else.

And yet, who doesn't love a bit of fury? That first line of Sam's "Dandelion". *Fury is my fuel now.* I would also draw your attention to Al again, with "Torn." How the language itself has been impacted by the energy of his Medusa muse. Read it again and you will feel what I mean.

> Curriculum directive: *This level is called Disquieting Muses. Ask yourself what muse energy is desperate for you to hear their siren song? They might be deceptive as they wind themself around your life and limb. Be patient, dig a little, invite them forward, yell or whisper the invitation that this is their time. Then get your pen ready.*

Jules Swales

PART VII

MUSE SEVEN

63

BENEATH THE SURFACE OF MY DULL

BY JB HOLLOWS

Beneath the surface of my dull, I feel the pressure of ancestors bear down on me.

I'm numb, empty, washed out, hung out to dry in a weak winter sun with no hope of air. Like my favourite old baggy blue jumper, worn to grey, threads just about hanging together.

The world waits.

Expecting.

Watching.

Judging.

The heavy dark cloak of despondency drags. My shoulders weigh down with life's demands. Unpaid bills wrap around ancient rocks and hang from huge, linked chains all over the fabric of my life.

Worry scratches my scarred arms. Doubt burrows poisoned arrows into my heart. Dread sheens me sweat.

Traffic sounds drum my ears, outwit the sound of my heartbeat, taunt my tender nose with fumes.

Robotic drivers cling to their stiff lives; feet pressed hard to the gas, getting nowhere, faster. Radios drown out space, drown out time, drown out God.

Lorries flick shiny carriages; horns blast morning vibrations; gigantic rubber wheels tear up the tarmac. Fear of the scrap heap disappears in the greed of man.

Sports cars laugh with diesel chocked pipes as fake leather seats caress neat, waxed arses. Pointy red nails, Botox lips, and rock-solid tits withstand the G-Force.

Tears flow from my midnight eyes.

Flow with rivers of pink salmon and brown bears. Flow with fresh water from lush forests. Flow despite myself, my failed life, my shrivelled powers, my daunting task.

The morning sky packs up her sunrise, spreads a blanket of pale blue and readies for the busy day.

A fox streaks across the green field between my tormented mind and the Zombie motorway. Bushy fur glints red. Undergrowth scents twitch her black nose. Alert charcoal eyes see the tiniest movement. Warm young pups squeal in their den, anticipating her return.

A bird darts from tree to tree. Flash of brown and white feathers. A fat worm dangles from his yellow beak. Scrawny young chicks squawk in twig entwined nests.

A bee burrows into the swollen buds of lusty flowers. Drinks deep gulps of sweet nectar. Sticky feet gather seeds to spread far and wide. Queen waits in her buzzing hive.

I breathe relief into the world through a long, deep, raspy sigh. The knot loosens in my strained throat. Blood fills the rose on my cheek, the cherry on my mouth, the pout on my lips.

The world turns another day.

64

MIDNIGHT SOUP

BY MER MONSON

I am alone, at last. Standing at the hearth with my feet planted in the warm wooden floor, I stir my midnight soup of stars. Burdock root and onion, garlic and butternut. Serenity, salt and solitude.

The stench of seriousness is buried and gone. The bones of fear are dust in the sky. No more illusion. No more fluff. No more authority. No more handcuffed obedience. No more intestines twisted around a crucible of guilt. No more suits and silent dresses to smother the smell of Mother Earth standing naked in the garden. The dawn hits Her like a prism, showering in circles on the glassy water. Her fire glows in the deep valleys of my skin, muscling the cacophony of testicle-flavored right-eousness to its knees. Only the arms of the trees are righteous here, where the flavor of God is always on my tongue. She is stir-ring my veins, stirring my blood, stirring my holy soup.

I stir for the weary until they are ready to come. They will come. They will swim to the limits of their longing. They will fall down, empty their bodies and let their clothes of heaviness fall. I will not force them to open their mouths, but my ladle waits, steaming and tipped, ready to pour the golden juice down into their hungry bellies.

Fullness bubbles over the edge of the pot and onto my speckled feet. It rises up to the cradle of my hips, fills my belly and chest, and rivers out my fingers. I wave my arms to make it dance. This body is free, a hawk that spreads and lifts on a whim. No resistance. No ache. No fight. Only love, in wrinkled grins, free to laugh and cry and dance and roar as I sprinkle the world with my womb of diamonds.

Lifetimes of souls breathe easy in the hollow of my breast as I stir my soup of butternut stars with a spoon of fern and moonlight.

65

BRAVE LIKE A SOLDIER

BY LN SHEFFIELD

I'm brave like a soldier, yet Wisdom is my weapon of choice, loaded with trust. A trust that runs deep and gushes through my very core. I have a tale to tell. One that may make you perish and shiver, as I stand tall and sing from my heart.

I've learnt to put myself first in a selfish world. I've learnt to prioritise my heart. I've learnt to unleash my secrets from those dark chambers. I've learnt to be wise, like the old barn owl who hoots at midnight.

Being a victim is overrated, undercooked, misunderstood. I'm an explorer of life. I wait like a cat ready to pounce. I gaze at the stars and wonder what next. What will the night sky throw down for me. I'm eager and sharp. I have my weapons by my side. My full body armour to protect me. I'm blessed with so much love. I've spent a lifetime shredding the bullshit, batting off the killjoys like an avid tennis player, aiming and not missing a single ball. I want to learn. I want to feel. I want to experience it all. Lap it up like a dehydrated, thirsty dog after a long, hot walk.

I shuttle about in my world, learning, growing, blossoming. I'm an acquired taste. I will chisel out the darkest of secrets. I lend my ears to the world. I'm a chatterbox who likes to chase. I like to chase truth and I won't stop until I find it. It is the hidden treasure of life.

I'm brave, like a soldier. Bring your bucket and spade as we dig for truth. I promise the earth and I don't let up. I'm a badass. Give me your hand. I've found my diamond. It was buried deep and now it shines brighter than a crystal hit by a chink of sunlight.

I move towards resistance with a beating heart, and sweaty palms, but I never back away. I never leave without my gift. I'm a kindred spirit. Let's mix up a pot of love. For I have a lifetime of anger and hate to boil away. It smells foul. Yet my weapons of wisdom tell me love smells sweeter. Breathe it in. Take my hand, for I'm brave like a soldier.

66

THREAD OF THE MOON

BY AL MILLEDGE

I play on threads
I share with the Moon,
they fizz,
I want more.

I feel her drag my cells
through luminescent biomes
wrench my inner world
to and fro, until

I stop
surrender resistance
then she is just
all me

as I always was.
Me, who can do,
be, anything.
Me of tricks,

impression, connection.
Me of life, death, love,
of quiet.
Me an indistinguishable sock

in a machine wash —
wet, soapy, equal
all of it, thread.
Bare, thread.

67

KALI

BY N. VYAS

There was no turning back,
no forward momentum.
I trusted nothing, no one,
least of all myself.

I withered away
one wisp at a time.
I folded in
layer after layer,

year after year,
time after time.
I fused into the grey.
Joy stripped away,

it didn't exist,
an illusion I believed,
so it dissolved.
No one came to play.

Puzzles, books undone, unread,
untouched, unloved.
An unlived tapestry
with loose saffron threads

pulled and frayed with age.
Beyond blue twilight
lay a secret in stardust,
but I couldn't open its fortune.

With eyes alive,
the time arrived to listen and obey,
to let the crimson sunset whisper the way.
I followed her fiery descent.

Go downward, she said,
go inward toward the last glimmer
of light, dreams, and play.
Go. Yes, go that way.

68

BEYOND THE HEDGEROWS

BY LINDA PRITCHER

"I'll go. I'll go now," she said into the shadow stricken room. A rueful smile crossed her face, then vanished like an outed flame. Her lover lay limp and crosswise on the bed, head hanging over the side where she could no longer see his face. A torn and crumpled tissue, stained a pale crimson, nestled in the creased sheets. Her skirt straightened and her starched blouse tucked, she stared out the window at the once regimented, now untidy garden.

There, a baby carriage sat unattended, a dark-haired doll had fallen at its side. A teacup lay overturned on its broken saucer. A blanket patterned like a chessboard, had been spread out on the grass at the edge of a thick hedgerow, ready for a game to begin, with no chess pieces or players in sight. A spinning wheel tangled in long pale tufts of silvery yarn, stood next to a large rabbit topiary. The rabbit was holding a sword, its bright brittleness contrasted with the glossy green enveloping leaves.

Beyond the hedgerows, wildness beckoned a deep puzzle blue of imagined lushness. She stood swaying inside, without moving, almost without breathing. Rapunzel in a tower. Her lifeline of long hair, warped and twisted, was now wrapped, sleek and tight against her head, against all blows. There was no need of useless warranties on the promise of happy endings with leaden-footed princes. Those princes arrived too late to rescue her dreams from ruin. The cut paper dragons of her childhood had breathed their last long ago on the playroom floor, conquered at her feet like Nanny. Nanny, who she'd tied shrieking to a chair and set on fire countless times.

Now, a one-legged crow cawed out her name. The sun retreated, the moon rose, the night twisted into a spiraling scarlet thread. "Coming, Mother," she said, grabbing the crumpled tissue. She folded its pale crimson wetness and placed it neatly into her short-handled leather purse, beside the bone bleached chess pieces. There was no point in saying goodbyes.

As she turned from the window, the polished marble floor caught the sharp click of her heel. She reached the door and *vanished*.

69

THREADS OF THEIR SINS

BY DEL ADEY-JONES

The blood of Pagans, Druids and Celts run through my Welsh veins. I wander the barren moors gathering heather, bracken, and peat for my hearth. I tend to the sick with poultices, herbal remedies, tinctures, and potions. I bring new life to barren wombs. I give sight to the blind and relieve the gout of a rich man's over-indulgence.

I've been branded a scarlet woman, a sinner, a sorceress, and spellbinder. I dance naked around standing stones. I howl into the wind, severing the threads of cosmic ties. I lay sacrifices on the gilded altar of the sacred Goddess. I raise my sword in praise and exaltation to all the directions. Mother Earth, Father Sky, Grandfather Sun, and Grandmother Moon. I bow and give thanks to my ancestors. My mother, my grandmother, and her mother before that.

There have been stories written about me, all nonsense, I swear. Never fear, your children are safe around me. I won't drink their adreno-chrome blood to retain my youth. I wish them no harm. I am their teacher, their guardian, their savior.

The accusers are wrong. So quick to judge what they don't understand. I only wreak havoc and revenge for the wrongs done to the innocent, weak, and infirm.

I poison the rapist's drink. I paralyze pedophiles into impotence. I tear out the eyes, ears, and tongues of murderers. I curse only those who have cursed me. I am master of my craft.

The lines of my face like the rings of an ancient tree. Markers of the passages of time spent wondering between celestial planes. You cannot destroy me, exorcise or drown me. I have withstood trials and tribulations. The smell of my burning flesh shall not stop me. My spirit lives on. I am eternal.

70

HAGIO

BY SAMANTHA HERMAN

I have been watching too much news, flicking between channel after channel, horror drying my mouth, fury rocking my head. Sun filled naps beckon, the stupor-inducing antidote to the staccato attack of life pandemic style.

I observe it all, not head burying, but rather a silent spectator at my own place in the experiment. The simple truth is we are born, therefore we die. We are here to be recycled. I was born on a black black evening, when even the stars hid, the night was so cold. But I am of no real interest here. Ancient energies can be submerged, but they never disappear.

If we choose to accept this truth, here are some points for consideration; why the urge to hold on, why the scramble for power, why then the resistance in every moment, the need to build, to create things that create money. Nonsense, money is anti-creator. It is removed from alchemy, the beauty, the true nature of this dance. Let me offer an alternative. I, and all of my ilk, can gift peace and succor. Inside this passing moment are the keys to infinity. Benevolence is my nature, but with benevolence comes reckoning. The bill must be paid. I cannot withhold understanding, but a price must be settled. That is the cycle, so long forgotten, subsumed in biblical notions of right and wrong.

The truth is in nature, a positive begets a negative, the atomic pull of creation, contraction and expansion. I suggest that you may find a way to live in spite of death. A bastion to hold on to beyond the concrete and so called scientific 'reality' that existence has been corralled into. To let go of illusions of greatness, a distraction frequently pursued, surrendering the fancy that destiny can be controlled, that death can be cheated, to cease believing that we can bend and shape fate by will, by brute force, by dominion and ignorant sacrifice of other. Just look at the destruction being played out on our beautiful, irreplaceable mother earth. The falsehoods we all pay the price for.

Follow me beyond the now, beyond the moment, the only beyond. Let me help you to surrender. Explode yourself. Explode to allow your essence to escape the battlements of security and a warm bed. Return to the mother, the truth, the gift long embedded in your heart.

71

WHO HOLDS THE THREAD?

BY MARIA ILIFFE-WOOD

Fear is a tight knot that waits to be unravelled. It's the undoing that scares me. I've been bound by this thread called control for so long, I fear its loss. If I don't hold myself together, who will?

A memory comes to mind. A day at the cemetery not long after my dad died. I was seated on a cold wooden bench set to the side of a bronze plaque that was all that was left of him. My head was tilted back, my neck stretched long, my auburn hair flowed down my back. My arms were spread wide open in supplication, hypnotised by the blue sky and the feather clouds that hung in the air. I imagined a polished steel knife as it slit my exposed throat and severed my mind from my body. No distress, nor bloody mess, just a sweet bliss.

I welcomed the end of the grief that had ripped at my heart. Grief, I thought would never stop. Grief that wreaked havoc on every cell in my body. Grief that I didn't realise would come and go of its own volition.

I experienced a peaceful departure from my existence, a love that enveloped me when I let go, an eternal stillness beyond the present moment.

The logical part of me knew this manner of death would not be as kind as it purported to be. Yet something died that day.

Something loosened and fell away. Something cracked me open, and all that was left was a calm residue.

I stood up from the bench and gathered my grief, along with an empty black rucksack, the contents of which now decorated the graves of three people I'd loved and lost.

Maybe I'm ready to let go. Maybe it won't be as painful as I think it will be. Maybe it's loose baggage I've got used to carrying around and its purpose is no longer valid. Maybe I need to die again, so that I can live. Maybe it's not me that holds the thread.

72

DIVINE FEMININE

BY LINDA SANDEL PETTIT

"Mama, I can't breathe," she said. Ancient and black, ankles spilled over battered sneakers, she raised her arms to the mystery.

Mystic vision, witch vision, warlock vision: sixth sight is her portal. She is discerned with the Third Eye, the eye between the eyes, the eye of the Soul. She is formless and eternal. She is the Divine Feminine.

I caught her eye this morning in a crystal pool, the bathroom mirror. Hair dyed auburn and spiked with sleep, a dead give-away to the Pippi Longstocking embedded in her bones—outrageous, unconventional, no parents to tell her what to do and a horse who lived on her porch. Cross her not.

Freckled face wrinkled and puffy, Broom-Hilda in a generous body, fifteen-hundred years old and still man-crazy. Cross her not.

Turquoise eyes, a muddle of ocean blue and healing green river. Turtle medicine. Gaia on her back. Cross her not.

Taupe robe cinched at the waist. Her breasts sagged like a tired mattress. Caffeine-starved in the pristine morning, she dared not cross herself. Cross her not.

Orange clogs on her feet, pinned to the ground in a swirl of yellow sunshine and red fire. Snake medicine. Transformation written into her skin. Cross her not. The price is dear.

She's not physical beauty.

She's not a naked dance in the moonlight.

She's not the shake of legs steepled around unconscious lovers.

She's not crystals, and talismans, dangled from taut young necks.

She's not any of that and she's all of that and more.

She does not require activation.

Or affirmation. Or prayer. She just is.

She's the tremored kiss of the old woman on the parched lips of the old man, the tongue of life that tastes sweetness long after the juices of youth have dried.

She's the caress of the shriveled claw on the hand of a beloved at the threshold of death. She weeps in witness. Not in grief, but in gratitude for no more pain, no more sorrow, no more separation, no more life. Only love.

She's the wail of the wraith who begs mercy from the moon for an earth in hospice.

"I'm Speaking," she declared to the patriarchy that women feel. Her generous power let down through unapologetic nipples.

With a wicked smile, I winked at her apparition in the glassine surface. I said, "Good morning, Divine Feminine."

EPILOGUE - CRONE/HAG/WITCH, WIZARD/SAGE

Webster's definitions:

Crone, a woman who is old and ugly.

Hag, an ugly, slatternly, or evil-looking old woman.

Witch, a woman thought to have magic powers.

Wizard, a wise man skilled in magic.

Sage, wise through reflection and experience.

If you are not of a seasoned age, do not think for a second you cannot write this muse. Of course, you can. Just like you can write the Mother muse whether you had a mother or not, or whether or not you've had a child.

I believe in past lives, in the fact that sometimes I feel wise beyond my years, that some energy stronger than I am is at play. Some might call this God, others Allah. For some, it is Spirit or the Essence of life. And even if none of that rings true, I know that all of us have a wisdom beyond our intellect.

So, no copping out before you even start with this muse. And to reiterate what I hope has become apparent, this muse class is not literal. There is a subtle dance at play where we listen less to our intellect and more to the energy of our body while maintaining the presence of each.

The archetypes/muses can also be regarded as personified symbols of various human qualities. Like the major arcana cards of the Tarot, they stand for the aspects of a complete human personality. Every good story reflects the total human story, the universal human condition of being born into this world, growing, learning, struggling to become individual, and dying. Stories can be read as metaphors for the general human situation with characters who embody universal archetypal qualities, comprehensive to the group as well as the individual. Christopher Vogler - The Writer's Journey

I think Vogler's words are so important. He is showing us the power and texture of Joseph Campbell's *The Hero's Journey*. And what a poignant time to reflect on that as we take a look at the Crone/Wizard pieces.

Let's start with Maria's "Thread" piece. It offers so much for the reader to explore, notwithstanding this splendid line: *I imagined a polished steel knife as it slit my exposed throat and severed my mind from my body.* And to the end, Linda Pettit's "Divine Feminine." When you read this, think back to her piece, "Don't Cross Me," in the Medusa chapter. Go back and read it. Then read this one. They are intrinsically linked. When I read the last line in this piece, I felt the energy ripple through my body! *Good morning, Divine Feminine.*

Definition: *Energy*: The capacity for vigorous activity, available power, an adequate or abundant amount of power, a feeling of tension caused or seeming to be caused by an excess of such power.

Jules Swales

OTHER BOOKS IN THE SERIES
METHOD WRITING WITH JULES SWALES

A Different Story: How Six Authors became Better Writers

ACKNOWLEDGMENTS

My first thanks go to Jules Swales, without whom this book would not exist. Not only is Jules a wonderful teacher of Jack Grapes' method writing, she is an ongoing support and cheerleader for all of her students. Without her, the authors in this book would not write as well as they do, and many would not have dared to offer their writing to be featured.

A thank you also goes to every author who has contributed their muse pieces for this publication. For many it was a scary proposition. I am delighted that so many fabulous writers trusted the feedback from their peers and Jules, and not their judgmental thinking about their writing.

I must thank Jack Grapes' for having come up with this wonderful way of learning how to find our unique and deep voice, and a way to create texture and dynamics in our writing. It is amazing how every exercise draws something new and fresh into one's writing.

I have had so much help and support from my project team, Jules Swales, Jacqueline (JB) Hollows and Jamie Fiore Higgins. It has been an amazing journey and it astounds me how the four of us together can make something so much greater than the sum of our individual parts.

Jacqueline thank you for your eternal enthusiasm for the book, and the meticulous attention you pay to the detail needed in the background to make this a success.

Jamie was to be one of the authors in the book, but due to her commitment with Simon and Schuster, she took a step back from being a contributing author, yet she still chose to play a huge part behind the scenes to help bring this book into the world. Thank you Jamie.

Our beautiful cover art was supplied by Renuka O'Connell. Thank you for not batting an eyelid when we asked if we could tamper with your original artwork to come up the perfect image to depict the androgynous nature of the Muses.

Thank you to Steve Pitcher at 18 Design, for the cover design.

A NOTE ABOUT ROYALTIES

Author royalties from this book will go to support those who want to share their story of redemption, so others can benefit, but who are in financial hardship. The royalties will help towards the cost of services required to publish a book. This could include the funding of places on IW Press programs to help them to write their book, or to pay for editing services, market research, interior formatting, cover design and other costs associated with getting a book out into the world.

ABOUT OUR AUTHORS

Jules Swales

Jules Swales is a British born poet and writer who studied Method Writing for over 18 years with her mentor Jack Grapes. She transitioned from the corporate world to teach the first online version of Method Writing with a desire to bring the power of the writing program to the world.

Jules is known for her poetry book, *I Want A Stonehenge Life*, but has also written a non-fiction book, and has been published in various journals and collections.

Jules volunteered at Venice High School where she taught Method Writing to the students in the POPS program. She has MA in Spiritual Psychology and also works one-on-one with clients as a Creativity Coach.

www.julesswales.com

instagram.com/julesswales/

Maria Iliffe-Wood

Maria Iliffe-Wood is the author of *Coaching Presence, Building Consciousness and Awareness into Coaching Interventions*, and *Daily Yarns: Riding the Lockdown Roller Coaster of Emotions*. She also contributed to and published *A Different Story*, the first book published through her company IW Press Ltd.

She uses skills gained as an executive coach for over 30 years, to coach and motivate people to write and publish their best book. She always has several book projects on the go. Her next book – A Caged Mind – is due to be published in summer 2022. She continues to be a student of Jules Swales.

www.iliffe-wood.co.uk
www.meridianiliffe.co.uk
facebook.com/iliffewood/
instagram.com/iliffewood/
linkedin.com/in/maria-iliffe-wood-52682912/

JB Hollows

JB Hollows MSc FRSA is an eclectic writer of creative nonfiction, short stories and academic research. Jacqueline plays with words and content creation to tell stories that inspire, motivate and make people think about the world in a different way. Works to date include: co-author of the first book in this series: A Different Story; co-author of several academic research papers; and a monthly column for a prison newspaper (the Insidetimes). JB is publishing her memoir in 2022, of her time as founder for a social enterprise working with prison inmates. JB is passionate about giving a voice to the voiceless and ending stigma.

www.beyond-recovery.co.uk
www.jbhollows.co.uk
instagram.com/beyonrecovery/
facebook.com/JBHollows
linkedin.com/in/jacqueline-hollows-beyond-recovery/

Del Adey-Jones

Del Adey-Jones is a Codependency and Narcissistic Abuse Recovery Coach, YouTuber and Blogger, and founder of A Spiritual Solution to Codependency and Narcissistic Abuse. She is host of the Insightful Conversations Podcast, and co-author of the book, Complete Self-Care... 25 Tools for Goddesses.

Thanks to her unconventional childhood and personal challenges including divorce and raising children as a single parent, her work is informed by her real-life experience and deeper studies of Spirituality and Psychology.

Using her down-to-earth, relatable approach to coaching and her commitment to creating a safe space to explore the Inside Out Understanding, she serves a wide range of clients worldwide.

www.deladeyjones.com

instagram.com/insightful.conversations/

facebook.com/Del-Adey-Jones-Coaching-112618520372588

linkedin.com/in/del-adey-jones-35a0543b

youtube.com/channel/UCPiJVkF16cp8ERXt3FvSK1Q

youtube.com/channel/UCTD-b5MzV9clXH2p5ah0C5A

Samantha Herman

Samantha Herman practised energy healing, counselling and psychotherapy for many years before deciding to focus her time on writing prose, poems and stories which reflect her varied experiences. She is an avid gardener and cook and addicted reader of many genres.

facebook.com/samantha.herman.754

Jennie Linthorst

Jennie Linthorst is the founder of LifeSPEAKS Poetry Therapy where she works with individuals exploring their personal histories through reading and writing poetry. She is on the faculty of UCLArts & Healing and presents workshops nationally including the East and West Coast Expressive Arts Summits. Jennie's poetry has appeared in Bluestem Magazine, Edison Literary Review, Foliate Oak, Forge, Kaleidoscope, Literary Mama, and more. Her poetry books are Silver Girl and Autism Disrupted: A Mother's Journey of Hope. Jennie has an M.A. in Spiritual Psychology, and certification in poetry therapy.

www.lifespeakspoetrytherapy.com.

https://www.facebook.com/LifeSPEAKSPoetryTherapy

https://twitter.com/JL_LifeSPEAKS

https://www.linkedin.com/in/jennie-linthorst-5a8a5624

Al Milledge

Al Milledge is an innate health coach and writer. He works as a teacher and coach in prisons and the LGBTQ community as well as with CEOs and professionals. He's passionate about ending unnecessary suffering by guiding people back towards their innate mental health, making space for them to bring something innovative into the world.

Al's been a student of method writing since 2018 and has led creative writing classes for men. He's still fascinated how this style of writing can bring out some of the most well-hidden, undiscovered parts of a writer, to allow them to be everything they are within an expansive and cathartic process.

www.alanmilledge.com

facebook.com/alan.milledge1

twitter.com/alanmilledge

Linkedin.com/in/alanmilledge

Mer Monson

Mer Monson fell in love with spilling her interior world onto the page during an adventure with cancer, and seven years later she's still hooked. She is the author of Reality Bathed in Hope: A Cancer Blog and has studied Method Writing since 2018.

As a Certified Master Transformative Coach with an M.S. in Psychology, Mer plays in the transformative space with clients all over the world through coaching, writing, speaking and podcasting.

She lives among a pile of half-read books and, at present, is being taken by the writings of Christian mystics.

www.mermonson.com

facebook.com/merrianne.monson/

www.instagram.com/mermonson/

Vanessa Poster

Vanessa Poster, a member of the Los Angeles Poets and Writer's Collective and the Poetry Salon, studied Method Writing with Jack Grapes for more than 20 years. Her work has appeared in Grief Dialogues, The Thieving Magpie, ONTHE-BUS, I'll have Wednesday, Went to Ralphs to Get a Chicken, and Fourth & Sycamore. She has been teaching creative writing since March, 2017 and runs a workshop called, "The Write Way: Using the Written Word to Heal." She is a graduate of Stanford University. She was widowed in 2015 and her poems explore themes of grief, love, and gratitude.

www.VanessaPoster.com

linkedin.com/in/vanessa-poster-9725b11

Linda Pritcher

Linda Pritcher has always been a creator of things - a visual artist, designer, entrepreneur and a writer. She's designed everything from billboards to high end shoes. Now she's being upstaged by the characters she's created in her first novel, which she's deep into the shady weeds of writing. When all that gets to be too much work, she'll settle down in front of a juicy classic film noir.

Somewhere between a down-and-out, misanthropic screen writer and the heroine of fantasy adventure novels is where Linda's mind resides. She's delighted to be among the authors in this unique book.

www.lindapritcher.com

facebook.com/Linda.Pritcher/

twitter.com/LindaPritcher

instagram.com/lindapritcher/

linkedin.com/in/lindapritcher/

Linda Sandel Pettit Ed.D

Linda Sandel Pettit guides women to own intuitive wisdom, claim spiritual power, and unbutton courage to live wild, wonderful, and free.

Linda integrates her understanding of intuitive spirituality with her experiences, accrued over 35 years, as a counseling psychologist, counselor, and scholar.

An unbuttoned woman with a passion for self-expression, Linda loves to help women share from their deep truth. She nurtures authentic voices, both spoken and written, through individual consultations, small group programs and copywriting services.

Find Linda's creative nonfiction blog and a description of her services on the web at:

www.lindasandelpettit.com

www.thedrspettit.com

facebook.com/thewildintuitivewayoflove

facebook.com/DrsPettit

instagram.com/lindasandelpettit/

instagram.com/lmspettit/

linkedin.com/in/linda-sandel-pettit

Anna Scott

Anna Scott is a lifelong learner. Along her journey she received a black belt in Aikido, a brown black belt in Kuk Sool and many Coaching Certificates from Strozzi Institute, Embodied Leadership, EpiGenetics and The Three Principles.

Recently Anna began writing with Jules Swales. She has taken what she learned from all her training dives into the space within, the space where creative genius lives.

www.annascott.co

facebook.com/anna.scott.3745

instagram.com/annascottcoaching/

LN Sheffield

LN Sheffield is a magical writing coach, children's fantasy author & an intuitive abstract artist. She has published two books, co-written two books and helped others publish their work.

On a day to day basis Lucy helps female professionals go from an under confident writer to a published author, step by step through her eight month programme.

Lucy has always had a passion for creativity. She expresses this through her love of writing & art. Lucy helps female professionals to find their own unique voice and share their message with the world through writing their book.

www.writingfromwisdom.co.uk
www.facebook.com/lucy.sheffield.16/
facebook.com/writingfromwisdom
www.instagram.com/sheffieldlucy/
twitter.com/LucySheffield3
linkedin.com/in/lucy-sheffield-63270574/

Sharon Strimling

Sharon Strimling is a writer, coach and speaker who lives with her partner and pup on a quiet island in a beautiful corner of the world. Smitten by nature and mystery, she writes to both, fumbles through them, falls into them. She tells of tall grasses and pounding waves, the noise of the mind and the quiet of the heart. Inspired by her and her clients' mental health journeys, Sharon writes to the brilliance beneath our shadows, and invites the voices of our full humanity – not when better, brighter, saner or wiser; but now. Perfectly imperfect, welcome and necessary.

www.sharonstrimling.com
linkedin.com/in/sharon-strimling/
facebook.com/sharonstrimlingcoaching
www.instagram.com/sharonstrimling/

N. Vyas

N. Vyas is a wanderer, explorer, mystic, who uses the written word to illuminate the richness of her inner world into the outer. Her past studies include an M.B.A. from the University of Chicago and an M.A. in Spiritual Psychology with an emphasis in Consciousness, Health & Healing. She blends the East and West into her work as a mentor, guide, and facilitator. N. lives with her husband in Park City, Utah, traveling often to visit her tribe scattered around the globe. She is delighted to participate in this work centered on archetypal energies with her fellow friends and writers.

linkedin.com/in/neha-vyas-918177/

Renuka O'Connell (Cover Artist)

Renuka O'Connell lives in Brunswick, Maine where she maintains a studio. She is an artist, writer and visionary coach. She owned an award winning Handcraft Arts Gallery for 30 years in Boston. Several of her paintings have been selected for social institutions. Her work has been shown in six art museums and one work is in the permanent collection of the Maine State Museum.

Her writing, painting, and assemblages explore the pure joy of discovery. She's a student of Method Writing and is working on a book project that combines the written word with her art.

www.renuartist.com

BIBLIOGRAPHY

- Method Writing: The First Four Concepts by Jack Grapes
- Advanced Method Writing by Jack Grapes
- The Writer's Journey by Christopher Vogler
- Collected Poems (1939) The Figure a Poem Makes by Robert Frost
- Wild Geese by Mary Oliver
- Webster's Dictionary - for all dictionary definitions.

CPSIA information can be obtained
at www.ICGtesting.com
Printed in the USA
LVHW081915050522
717951LV00013B/336